RAW

EDGES

A RENEGADE JUSTICE THRILLER

CJ LYONS

Also By CJ Lyons:

Lucy Guardino Thrillers:
SNAKE SKIN
BLOOD STAINED
KILL ZONE
AFTER SHOCK
HARD FALL
BAD BREAK
LAST LIGHT

Hart and Drake Medical Suspense:
NERVES OF STEEL
SLEIGHT OF HAND
FACE TO FACE
EYE OF THE STORM

Shadow Ops Covert Thrillers:
CHASING SHADOWS
LOST IN SHADOWS
EDGE OF SHADOWS

Fatal Insomnia Medical Thrillers:
FAREWELL TO DREAMS
A RAGING DAWN
THE SLEEPLESS STARS

Angels of Mercy Medical Suspense:
LIFELINES
WARNING SIGNS
URGENT CARE
CRITICAL CONDITION

Caitlyn Tierney FBI Thrillers:
BLIND FAITH
BLACK SHEEP
HOLLOW BONES

RAW EDGES

A Renegade Justice Thriller

CJ Lyons

EDGY READS

Note to Readers:

Thanks for joining in on Morgan's adventures in the Renegade Justice thrillers! This book, RAW EDGES, is a sequel to her first adventure in FIGHT DIRTY, but can be read on its own.

Morgan will be back in 2017 with a new story, ANGELS WEEP, which begins immediately after the ending of RAW EDGES.

(Want to be the first to know when new stories are coming, join us on my Thrillers with Heart mailing list at www.CJLyons.net)

A note to those who are also fans of the Lucy Guardino Thrillers: the Renegade Justice stories take place in the year between Lucy's adventures in KILL ZONE and AFTER SHOCK.

The complete chronology for those who enjoy reading in order is:

SNAKE SKIN: Lucy Guardino FBI Thrillers #1

BLOOD STAINED: Lucy Guardino FBI Thrillers #2 (Morgan and Jenna are introduced as well as Clinton Caine)

KILL ZONE: Lucy Guardino FBI Thrillers #3 (features Morgan and Jenna; Andre is introduced)

FIGHT DIRTY: Renegade Justice Thrillers, featuring Morgan Ames #1

RAW EDGES: Renegade Justice Thrillers, featuring Morgan Ames #2

ANGELS WEEP: Renegade Justice Thrillers, featuring Morgan Ames #3 (coming 2017)

AFTER SHOCK: Lucy Guardino FBI Thrillers #4

HARD FALL: Lucy Guardino FBI Thrillers #5

BAD BREAK: Lucy Guardino FBI Thrillers #6

LAST LIGHT: Beacon Falls Mysteries, featuring Lucy Guardino #1

DEVIL SMOKE: Beacon Falls Mysteries, featuring Lucy Guardino #2

OPEN GRAVE: Beacon Falls Mysteries, featuring Lucy Guardino #3 (releases February, 2017)

If you enjoy Morgan's adventures and want more, please leave a review!

Thanks for reading,

CJ

PS: want advance notice of new books and the chance for exclusive prizes and behind-the-scenes info? Join the Thrillers with Heart newsletter at www.CJLyons.net

CHAPTER 1

DR. NICK CALLAHAN missed his wife. Yet, as lonely as his empty house was with Lucy and their daughter, Megan, gone to visit his parents in Virginia, Nick was glad Lucy wasn't there. Now, for the fourth morning in a row, he ate his breakfast, showered, dressed, set the newly installed alarm, and drove to his office, a not-so-discreet unmarked police car trailing close behind.

Nothing like a psychopathic serial killer escaped from prison to help put your priorities in order, he thought as he waved to the guard at the VA's security desk and used his ID badge to gain access through the two sets of locked doors between the main entrance and his office in the counseling center. Usually he'd be working out of his private office on a Friday, but the police—and Lucy—had convinced him to reschedule his patients to the VA, given its greater security.

It was a bit embarrassing, explaining to his clients why they had to drive to the VA for their sessions, but the majority of his patients were military and law enforcement, and to a one, they had understood. Still, he felt silly. No way in hell would Clinton Caine target Nick. Given the manhunt focused here in the Pittsburgh area and the surrounding western Pennsylvania countryside, Caine would have a lot more to keep him occupied than any thoughts of vengeance on family members of the FBI agent who'd caught him.

Nick smiled as he turned the doorknob to his office. It was a private smile usually reserved for his wife, but of course Lucy wasn't here to see it. Still, he couldn't help but feel a sense of pride. She'd caught Caine not once, but twice.

The man would have to be a fool to even think of coming after Lucy or targeting her family.

"I need your help," a woman's voice greeted him from inside his dark office.

Startled from his private reverie, Nick jumped—and immediately covered it by stumbling to turn the light on, revealing his unexpected guest. Not a woman, a girl.

He knew better than to ask how Morgan Ames had gained access to his supposedly secure office. Morgan had an uncanny ability to be able to go wherever she damned well pleased. Part social engineer extraordinaire, part master hacker, and part cat burglar, the skills served her well when she'd been working with her father, Clinton Caine.

"Is it your father?" Nick asked, dropping his voice until he had the door closed behind him, even though no one else was here yet, not this early on a Friday morning.

Morgan shook her head. She looked miserable.

On the surface, she was dressed like

a young executive, someone from a glossy magazine cover. Made up to look like she was in her twenties, even though he knew she was only fifteen—or at least that was the age she'd finally claimed. Who knew what the truth really was when it came to Morgan?

Despite appearing impeccably ready for the world, he saw through her mask effortlessly—another warning sign that things were very, very wrong. Dark circles hid beneath her makeup, and when she stood to begin pacing, her gait was agitated instead of the well-balanced, always ready-to-strike poise she usually exhibited. Gone was her preternatural aura of calm command—an aura that always reminded him of Lucy, truth be known.

"What is it, Morgan?" he asked, using his most reassuring tone.

"I can't sleep," she finally admitted. "Haven't for days." Restless energy sparked from her as she stalked the room, weaving around his desk, the couch, coffee table, and two chairs. "At first I wasn't trying to sleep, was busy

4

setting up security measures, watching for Clint, but then, when I tried..." Her voice trailed off with an uncertainty that was alien to the Morgan he knew.

"Can you tell me why? What's keeping you awake?" Morgan could sleep anywhere, anytime; since she didn't feel anxiety about the events of the day, there was never anything to keep her awake, worrying like normal people. One of the many reasons why she considered her sociopathy as not a diagnosis of maladjustment but rather a sign of superiority.

"No. Can't you see? That's the problem, I can't explain it." The words gnashed free from her clenched jaws.

Nick had never seen Morgan like this—usually he had to push to force her to feel any emotions, much less acknowledge them. "You've mentioned the mania you sometimes experienced when you participated in your father's activities."

Every fiber of his being cringed at the thought of what Clinton Caine's activities had included: stalking and abducting women, using his own children as bait; taking his victims to remote locations where he'd imprison, torture, and rape them until they bore children of their own—his children. Caine had been desperate for a family, one that would obey him and feed his desire for pain.

Nick had no idea where Caine's pathology stemmed from—from his own family, most likely—but the father had definitely warped and ruined his favorite daughter, turning Morgan into an inhuman killing machine. It was a testimony to Morgan that she'd been able to break away from that indoctrination by blood.

She prowled the room with jittery steps, a supernova ready to explode. "I wish I could make you feel it, understand." The words came at a stuttering pace. "It's nothing like what I felt with Clint. That was...gleeful. A rush of power. Nothing, no one, could stop us. We were our own gods." She spun to face him, the dark circles beneath her eyes making her appear haunted. "This, this is nothing like that. Back then with him, I'd stay up for days on the sheer thrill of adrenaline, but this...I've never felt like this, never."

"Okay, okay." He kept his voice soothing. "I've an idea. It might sound kind of weird, but work with me here."

"What?" Her gaze was heavy with suspicion. "No pills. I don't want any drugs messing with my head, especially not now with Clint loose. I need to stay sharp."

"No pills," he promised. "But we need to understand what's going on with you. If you can't sleep, you can't stop Clint."

She nodded at that. He motioned to the love seat, and she plopped down in it, acting for once exactly like the fifteen-year-old girl she was. Occasionally, after a meeting with Morgan and returning home to his own teenaged daughter, Nick mourned what could have been. Morgan would have been a remarkable, beautiful girl—if her father hadn't ravaged her childhood in such a brutal manner.

"Now what?" she asked.

He eased into the chair across from

her. "Now close your eyes."

She did but then immediately popped them open. "You're not going to try to hypnotize me?"

"No, nothing like that. I'm not going to do anything but listen. You're going to do all the work. Close your eyes."

Her expression was doubtful, but she did. It occurred to Nick that he was probably the only man on the face of the planet that Morgan would feel safe to drop her guard with. Well, maybe Andre Stone as well. The former Marine had won Morgan's admiration and respect. Two out of seven billion? The odds were stacked against her in so many ways. Even without a vicious serial killer on her trail.

"They're closed. What do I do now?"

"Now tell me about this feeling you have." She opened her mouth, but he continued before she could protest. "Not how it makes you feel. Instead, I want you to imagine the feeling come to life. Imagine it as a place or a scene, something you're doing. Don't try to put the emotion into words. Rather, find the place that feels the same and take a look around, notice every detail."

"Like what Micah does with his drawing?" Micah Chase was a boy whose life Morgan had saved. As much as Nick would love to get her to open up about her feelings for Micah, feelings he knew she hadn't even admitted to herself, giving her the skills she needed to cope with her father's escape from prison took priority.

"Exactly. Think of it as drawing a scene. What are you doing there? What's the weather like? What does it smell like? Who else is there with you?"

She hugged her arms tight around her chest, a self-comforting act he doubted she was even conscious of.

"Have you found your place?" he asked.

"Yes. It's cold, so cold. And dark." God, had she returned to one of her father's killing places? Many of them had been underground. He leaned forward, ready to redirect her, but she said, "Except the stars. I've never seen stars so bright. It smells like Christmas. Pine trees and snow."

"Where are you, Morgan?"

"I'm walking on water—a pond frozen over? It's so black, it's like I'm walking on the stars reflected in it. But I don't feel special or powerful enough to walk on water. Each step is an agonizing choice, the ice groaning, one wrong step and it will crack. It's too thin, too brittle. It can't protect me. No matter which way I turn, I'll step wrong." Despite her obvious fear, her voice remained calm, no panic—Morgan never panicked.

"Look up, Morgan. Do you see anything else?"

Her chin slid upward even as her eyes remained closed. "Oh God," she breathed out, anguish filling her voice. "They're all here. Because of me. I brought them here."

"Who? Who's with you, Morgan?"

"All of them. Micah, Andre, Jenna, you...not Lucy." Her forehead frowned. "Why not Lucy?"

He didn't want to color her visualization, but her instincts were correct: Lucy had stopped Clinton Caine twice already; she had little to fear from him. And Caine was smart enough to stay far, far away from giving Lucy a third chance to put him down like the rabid dog he was. "What are the others doing?"

She shook her head, avoiding his question. "No. No. They shouldn't be here. But they came. Because of me." Her hands fisted, raised as if fighting an unseen force. "The ice, it's too thin. It's groaning under the weight, it's cracking. I can't stop it, I can't help them." She gasped, hands flying up to cover her face. "It broke. Swallowed me whole, pulling me down into the dark, black cold, I can't breathe, I can't fight, I can't see the stars..."

She flew off the love seat and launched herself at him, eyes bulging with terror. She gripped Nick by the shoulders although from the expression on her face as she loomed over where he was trapped in his chair, he knew she'd rather have her hands around his neck. Progress.

"You lied," she accused him, her voice ratcheted tight with adrenaline. "You hypnotized me."

"No, no, I didn't." His voice was calm, professional. He fearlessly met her gaze. "You did it all on your own."

She released him and stepped back, glancing at the love seat as if surprised to find it still there and not drowned in the lake she'd conjured. "Was I dreaming? Did I fall asleep?"

"Not exactly. It was just an exercise in imagination. Some people aren't good with words, do a better job with images. You created an entire scene to describe the anxiety and dread you've been feeling but couldn't otherwise express or label."

"Dread." She tasted the word, grimacing. "Dread. Like there's someone or something stalking you, watching every breathing second, herding you toward some inescapable horror. And you're powerless. Can't stop, can't fight." She turned to Nick. "Is that dread?"

"As good a description as any. A pervasive feeling that something terrible is about to happen."

She shuddered. "How do you Norms survive? Walking around with all these emotions dulling your reflexes. No wonder you're sheep. Easy prey."

She didn't mean any insult with her words; they were simply Morgan's view of the world, colored by her upbringing and lack of empathy. The fact that she'd progressed to the point where she could feel dread or anxiety, much less the unconscious empathy she'd shown the other people present in her imagainary scene, gave Nick hope. Despite the fact that Morgan was the most damaged person he'd ever treated, maybe she still had a chance.

"Why were those people with you on the pond, Morgan?" he asked in a gentle tone.

She waved his words away with a hand. "Fools. Trying to play hero. I don't need their help." Her very presence here in his office exposed her lies, but she didn't seem to notice. "I won't let them."

"Won't let them help you?" Nick probed.

"Won't let them fall victim to Clint." She took in a deep breath, her gaze clear once more. A decision made. "Thanks, Nick. That helped."

"How so? We haven't come to the reason behind your feelings, merely given them a name."

"A name is all I need. I already know the reason." Her smile was not genuine— at least he hoped it wasn't, filled as it was with teeth and bloodthirsty glee. "All I have to do now is stop Clint. For once and for good."

CHAPTER 2

AFTER LEAVING NICK, Morgan approached the Galloway and Stone offices with caution. First, she parked the car she'd borrowed from the long-term lot at the Pittsburgh airport several blocks away from the office's Regent Square location. Then, she meandered down the sidewalk, taking her time as she glanced at the various art galleries and antique shops, occasionally wandering inside one. It was ten o'clock on a Friday morning, and most stores had just opened for business, leaving her their only customer—making it easy to spot anyone overly interested in her aimless browsing.

Finally, she got a coffee and checked her phone, scanning footage from the cameras she'd placed to spy on the office. Nothing. Was that good or bad? Her father had escaped from prison four days ago; his first act as a free man had been to call her and tell her he was coming for her, and yet...nothing.

Dread, Nick had called it. Should have never have gone to him, let him play his headshrinker games. Nick meant well, but he was used to treating Norms, not someone like Morgan. He didn't understand that it didn't matter what she felt or what label you gave it, all that mattered was the end result. She had to focus on that. Forget all the rest. Mumbo-jumbo feelings were for Norms, not Morgan.

She sipped at her coffee—wasn't sure if you could even call it coffee, she'd ordered some mocha-frothy nonsense that fit with the persona she was wearing, but it did taste pretty good. Not that that mattered, she'd simply needed the distraction for anyone watching the person they would see as a twenty-something blonde wearing dark blue slacks and a cowl neck beneath a hoping-for-spring pink wool coat. Appearances were everything.

The warm drink did its job, removing the chill of the late March morning. Although it definitely didn't ease Morgan's mind. She pocketed her phone, not sure whether to be worried or relieved at finding no signs of surveillance.

Dread. Never knowing when the blow could come or which direction it would come from. However you labeled it, Clint had perfected its creation. It'd been her father's unique signature in his former occupation of sadistic serial killer. She'd spent a large part of her life as the chief object of his emotional manipulation, but until now she hadn't fully appreciated how much freedom she'd enjoyed while he'd been behind bars.

And now Clinton Caine was free. Ready to pick up where he'd left off. Her mouth twisted as if the coffee had gone bitter.

"Something wrong, miss?" the barista asked, rubbing the March Madness promotional button she wore on her apron. The entire city was gearing up for the Pitt game tonight, especially as it was being held downtown at the Arena. Morgan could tell the woman took pride in her work, was genuinely worried. What luxury—having nothing more than coffee to worry about. It was difficult to even imagine.

Morgan rearranged her face into a bland smile. "No, nothing. I'm just running late."

"I like your coat. It's nice to see spring colors." She nodded to the grey March clouds that made it impossible to tell if it was morning or night—until the sun blazed through them, blinding drivers and pedestrians alike for a few wistful moments before vanishing faster than Punxsutawney Phil seeing his shadow. Typical schizophrenic Pittsburgh spring. Barely above freezing this morning, a high near sixty predicted, and they were calling for sleet and snow again tonight and tomorrow. March Madness indeed.

"Thanks." Morgan snuggled deeper into the soft wool of the ankle-length coat. She was certain the color had a pretty-girl name like rose cream or rose blush, and she'd only stolen it because it fit with the blond persona. Ordinarily, as herself, she'd never wear a coat that would attract attention like this one, but when you wanted people not noticing or remembering your face, sometimes a diversion like a pretty pink coat was necessary. If anyone ever asked, Morgan had practically crafted the barista's testimony for her: blond, early twenties, in a pretty pink coat, acted like a secretary or maybe a salesperson for one of the upscale Regent Square boutiques.

She finished her coffee, left a generous tip to further cement her persona, and left, the sun following her movements, breaking free of the clouds in a golden blaze.

Morgan reached for her sunglasses—her favorite fashion accessory. Who wouldn't like socially acceptable camouflage that allowed you to spy on others without revealing your own gaze? Not to mention sharp-edged lenses that could double as mirrors or cutting instruments, along with flexible lengths of wire perfect for picking locks or poking out an eye, depending on the needs of the moment. The ultimate survival tool, she'd wear her sunglasses day and night if it were practical. In fact, the few times she'd played a persona who was blind, she had. It had been glorious, hiding in plain sight, the world unfolding before her, unwitting and vulnerable.

Clint had loved using her in the role of blind cripple, setting her to surveil a target. What do you see? he'd urge her. Look past the surface. Who do you see? What are they really? Can you see them? Can you really see?

She flinched against his seductive whisper but couldn't resist the urge to circle the block one last time, making sure there was no sign of Clinton Caine or any of the other two maximum security prisoners who had escaped with him. *You shouldn't be here,* his voice echoed through her mind. *You don't belong—*

unless you want me to find your friends? Pay them a visit?

The voice in her head might be his, but the doubts were hers and hers alone. She shouldn't be here—she should be halfway around the world by now. Far away from anyone she cared for, leading Clint even farther away from them. And yet...she'd tried to leave, twice she'd made it all the way to the state line, she'd told herself she could keep an eye on her friends from a distance, safer that way for everyone...and twice she'd turned back, returned to Pittsburgh.

Her first instinct—after running—was to hunt Clint alone. Find him, kill him, return to her life, and forget she ever had a father. But with the FBI, US Marshals, State Police, a handful of county sheriff's departments along with numerous local police departments searching for him and the other escapees and coming up empty, she realized she'd have to make him come to her. And somehow protect her friends while she did it.

Which meant coming home. This

morning's session with Nick had only served to cement her resolve.

It was the kind of plan that wasn't really a plan at all: embracing the dread, playing the role of sacrificial lamb, waiting for Clint to pounce. It was the kind of plan she hated. Morgan much preferred playing the role of the wolf stalking its prey rather than Judas goat.

But it was the only plan that would allow her to keep an eye on the people she cared about and make certain that if anyone was ensnared by Clint, it would be her, not them.

Scouring the approach to Jenna Galloway's building, nodding in approval at the two unmarked police vehicles watching the main entrance, she finally entered the ground floor art gallery, sidled into the narrow passage that led to the storage area, disarmed the lock, pushed through the door to the private stairwell, then jogged up the steps, one hand on the pistol in the pocket of her coat.

At the Galloway and Stone Security Consultants' door, she paused to remove her sunglasses and wig, shaking free her dark curls. Plastering on another disposable smile, she entered.

"About time you showed up," Jenna Galloway called from behind her desk in her office across from the reception area. "Figured you'd be hiding under a rock somewhere with your dad on the loose. Or halfway to Argentina."

That was Jenna being nice. Despite the fact that Morgan knew her deepest secrets and was the closest thing to a female friend Jenna had. Morgan didn't mind. She didn't need Jenna to like her, merely to be there when Morgan needed her. "Belize," she corrected cheerfully. "No extradition, and they speak English."

Andre Stone, Jenna's partner in business as well as in life, came barreling out of his office, paused for a brief second to scrutinize Morgan head to toe, then pulled her into a rib-crushing hug that lifted her from her feet. Surprising, because Andre knew the truth of who Morgan really was, including the fact that from the time she was a child, her father had forced her to participate in his torture and kidnappings as well as teaching her how to kill—and enjoy it.

Andre was a former Marine with his own battle scars—burns over sixty percent of his body accompanied by more difficult to heal psychic wounds—and he'd appointed himself Morgan's protector. By accepting her into his family, he'd place his life on the line for her. He'd also be the first to put an end to her if she returned to her violent ways, which made Morgan's relationship with Andre the most honest one she'd ever had in her life.

That was why, despite the fact that she despised being touched and had no clue how to offer affection in return— another problem with growing up being groomed by a serial killer—she not only tolerated Andre's embrace, she squeezed him back. Just like a normal person would.

During her sleepless vigil over the past few days, Morgan had questioned why she was so determined to even try to pretend to be normal. So far, it'd turned out to be hard work and a pain in the ass.

Except for one bright spot: Micah Chase. Morgan had met Micah when she'd gone undercover in a juvenile detention center. Although Morgan could pass for anything from twelve to twenty-something, she was actually only fifteen, so it'd been an easy role for her to play, exposing the corruption that had led to a girl's death.

But then she'd met Micah, a seventeen-year-old incarcerated through no fault of his own. Micah, like Andre, wasn't one of the many sheep that so many Norms were, mindlessly grazing through life. And he certainly was no fish—her father's word for his victims. Micah was a protector. He'd risked his own life to save Morgan's. He had no clue who or what she really was, yet she felt like she could tell him anything and he'd understand. Understand *her* like no one else did.

That scared Morgan. She'd never been to school or had any kind of normal friendships with kids her own age, and here was Micah, offering her the world. All she had to do was decide to accept what he offered.

She'd replayed their single kiss over and over in her mind. Ridiculous, really. She had a sadistic killer on her trail, no time to indulge in fantasies of being a normal adolescent girl. She had to take care of herself. No room to take care of anyone else.

Better to run from Micah as fast as she could—for his sake, if not hers.

For four days, that's what she told herself. Yet, each evening she'd found herself talking to Micah on the phone, watching him through the cameras she placed around the house he shared with his mothers, and wishing things were different.

Which was why she'd returned to Galloway and Stone, despite the fact that every instinct told her to run, run, run.

Chapter 3

Morgan hung up her coat, surprising herself with a wistful brush of her hand along its baby soft pink sleeve before turning to follow Andre into Jenna's office, which currently looked like a military campaign's war room. The desk was strewn with large-scale topographic maps, the walls and even the windows were plastered with notes and photos and random scraps of paper. All centered on one man: Clinton Caine.

"I'm glad you're finally back," Jenna said, leaning over her desk and stabbing a pin into one of the maps. "The reward for your father just went up to one hundred thousand. Fifty each for the brothers." Clint had been accompanied by two brothers, both serving life sentences, when he'd escaped from a prison transport van.

Morgan looked to Andre for sanity. He grimaced and shrugged as if helpless to control Jenna. Of course he was. Andre was in love with Jenna, and she used that against him any chance she had. Funny thing was, Jenna really did love Andre as well. In her own unique, narcissistic way.

"State and local police, the FBI and US Marshals are all searching for Clint. What makes you think you can do better?" Morgan asked.

"We have a secret weapon." Jenna tilted her head up from the map, her gaze drilling into Morgan. "You. If you've come back to work." Her words cracked through the air, a gauntlet being thrown down.

"I don't want anything to do with my father," Morgan lied. Jenna wanted to capture Clint, grab the glory, cash, and headlines. Morgan wanted him out of her life once and for all. If a maximum security prison cell couldn't hold him, a deeply dug grave would. "You shouldn't either. You know what he's capable of. Leave it to the pros."

Too late, Morgan realized her mistake. Jenna had once been a federal agent, working for the US Postal Inspector Service. She considered her skills as good as or better than "the pros."

"They've got squat, and it's been four days already," Jenna snapped. "But I have some leads. I need you to help me narrow them down."

"What kind of leads?" No way would Clint not cover his tracks.

"Jenna thinks your father will go after his money," Andre explained. "We know before he was caught that he had caches of cash and supplies hidden throughout the area he covered on his trucking route."

"We just need you to tell us where they are, and we'll take it from there." Jenna challenged Morgan with a stare as she handed her a pen. "After all, you are part of the Galloway and Stone team, right? This would be a big win for the firm."

Morgan didn't take the bait. Jenna lowered the pen. "Or maybe you're worried because you don't know where your father is. Did you come back so we can protect you from daddy dearest?"

"Jenna—" Andre's tone was one of admonishment.

"I left to protect you. I didn't want Clint to go after either of you, thinking he could get to me." It was true, but Jenna clearly didn't buy it. Andre did, though. He placed a hand on Morgan's shoulder and squeezed in encouragement.

"I came back," Morgan continued, "because I don't think my father is a threat. If he wanted me, he'd have already come after me." Another lie. She knew better than anyone how patient Clint could be when it came to baiting a hook and toying with his fish.

If Morgan couldn't leave, then sending Jenna and Andre on a wild goose chase would be the best way to keep them safe. She took the pen from Jenna. "I think you're right. He'll go after his money and then start over. Somewhere safe, another country maybe. Somewhere he can play his games without looking over his shoulder."

Only problem was, she'd already raided most of Clint's caches while he was in prison. Another reason for him to come after her. Clint was much too lazy to try to start over. He'd want Morgan and her skills; after all, she was the one who'd originally stolen the money needed to fund his fun and games. Plus, he'd be furious at her betrayal. He'd want—no, he'd need—to see her pay. Dearly and in person.

Jenna narrowed her eyes at Morgan, parsing her words, searching for the lie. But since Morgan had basically told her exactly what Jenna wanted to hear, she didn't work too hard at it. "Where should we start?"

Morgan scanned the map. Where would her father have already been and gone? Or better yet, not bother going at all? Places safe enough to send Jenna and Andre while she stayed here as bait.

She circled two spots—one an old

money cache, already emptied to pay for Clint's defense, which he well knew. The second a safe house he hadn't used in years, mainly food and weapons, little cash, nothing to draw Clint there. It was a cabin up on Tussey Mountain, difficult to get to on foot, impossible by any vehicle larger than an ATV.

Should be good enough to keep Jenna and Andre safely out of trouble for a few days, at least. In the meantime, Morgan was still working out how to set a trap for her father without being caught herself.

Problem was, he knew her too well—he'd basically created her, molded every aspect of her personality until she was his perfect foil. She had to find a way to make him come to her while thinking it was his idea, not hers.

Jenna squinted at the two spots Morgan had indicated. "Middle of nowhere. What's there?"

Morgan tapped the first. "His bank—money cache. Probably already ransacked," she added. The best lies began with the truth. She jotted down

GPS coordinates and the combination to Clint's deposit box at the vault. "The second is a safe house. Hunting cabin, really. Only basic supplies. Hard to get to but easy to defend and multiple escape routes." She glanced at Jenna. "Pretty rough terrain."

"Think I can't handle a few trees?" Jenna asked. "I've been camping."

Even Andre scoffed at that. Jenna's style of "camping" no doubt included a designer wardrobe from Abercrombie and Fitch along with catering from the nearest four-star restaurant.

Jenna glanced up, and he wiped the smirk from his face. "Well, I have. But always start with the money. Fugitive Tracking 101. Besides, the money cache is closer."

The phone rang. Jenna continued her study of the map. Andre grabbed it. "Galloway and Stone." He listened for a few minutes. "Yes, ma'am. No, of course. We'll be there."

He hung up. "Clinton Caine will have to wait," he told Jenna. "It's Mrs. Radcliffe, confirming our appointment."

Jenna frowned. "Her, again? I thought we turned her down."

"A new case?" Morgan asked.

"Missing sixteen-year-old boy. His mother wants us to consult, augment what the police are doing."

"Probably out partying or with a girl," Jenna said, still focused on the map. Morgan thought she was probably right— just as she recognized that this new case was Andre's way of trying to divert Jenna from the hunt for Clinton Caine.

"Gone almost a week. She sounds desperate."

Jenna rolled her eyes. "Don't they all? That's why they call us."

Andre blew his breath out with a raspy sound of exasperation. "And isn't that why we're in business?"

"I need to work these new leads on Caine. Take Morgan." She sat down and opened her laptop, dismissing them.

Andre stared at Jenna, a crease forming beneath the ridge of scar tissue along his forehead. Disappointment, Morgan recognized—despite his scars, he was in many ways easier to read than other Norms. But he shrugged it off and turned to her. "What do you say, Morgan? You on board for another case?"

"Yes, sir, Mr. Stone." Morgan smiled at Andre—a real smile, not one of her endless supply of artificial ones. She loved that after their last case, he trusted her enough to invite her to join him, even if a large part of it was his desire to keep an eye on her.

Jenna would be busy following her wild-goose chase after Clint, and maybe this new case would give Morgan a chance to keep Andre occupied while she lured her father close enough to turn the tables on him.

CHAPTER 4

AFTER SEEING MORGAN and Andre off on their fool's errand, Jenna retreated to the office's back closet to gather supplies for her manhunt. Extra magazines of ammunition for her SIG Sauer P226, a second SIG along with an ankle holster, ballistic vest, field trauma kit, stun gun, box of slugs for her Remington pump action, two pairs of handcuffs, zip ties, more zip ties, and, from a space hidden behind the carton of zip ties, a box of her favorite coconut-chocolate protein bars...which was empty. Damn it, how did Morgan always find them?

She hung her vest on a hook and secured the items in their respective pockets. Then she shook the vest roughly, checking for any extraneous rattles, loose gear, weight, and balance. Once she was satisfied, she grabbed the vest along with the rest of her equipment and returned to her office.

Only to find a hulking man wearing a black windbreaker and a scowl that on second glance was maybe a weird interpretation of a grin standing in her doorway. "You're loaded for bear."

"How'd you get in?" she demanded, stalking over to her desk and dumping everything on top of the map to hide it. She casually laid a hand on her SIG, still in its holster. How'd he sneak up on her? Such a big guy, she should have heard him coming a mile away. Except he wasn't really that big, was he? Definitely not as tall as Andre, he just...felt big. With his Asian features, shaved head, massive shoulders. "Who the hell are you?"

"Oshiro. Timothy Oshiro. Deputy US Marshal." He pointed to the insignia on his windbreaker, but it was faded to the point of being barely legible. As he shifted his weight, the jacket fell open to reveal a ballistic vest and the distinctive circular silver badge with a star in the center clipped to a chain around his neck.

"Oshiro." She'd heard of him. "You're leading the FAST team." The Marshals service led multi-agency fugitive apprehension strike teams throughout the country. The one for Western PA had a particularly stellar success record.

"Yes, ma'am. Lucy Guardino thought I might find Morgan Ames here. As you can imagine, we'd appreciate a conversation with her. I understand she might have some insights into Clinton Caine. My men never saw her enter, but we spotted her leaving a little while ago with your associate, Mr. Stone, so I thought I'd come introduce myself."

"You're surveilling us?" Jenna wasn't certain whether to be outraged or relieved. Morgan had increased security around the building, and Jenna had added more herself, especially to the loft upstairs that she shared with Andre, but no amount of security could keep anyone safe from Clinton Caine.

"Seemed a good idea, given you and Lucy were the two responsible for Caine being locked up in the first place. Not to mention his daughter working here." He wrinkled his nose. "Can't find much of anything on her, we're not even sure of her exact age, but if she really is Clinton Caine's daughter, wouldn't she be a bit young to be assisting a pair of security consultants?"

She restrained herself from rolling her eyes. Of the three of them, Jenna, Andre, and Morgan, Morgan had the greatest real-life experience with criminal activity and thwarting security. Not that she'd ever admit that to Morgan's face. "Do you have people following her and Andre?"

"Yes. But right now, I'm more interested in where you're going."

It was strange. Oshiro hadn't moved from where he'd planted himself between the door and her desk, all he'd done was flick his eyes toward the map on her desk, yet Jenna felt compelled to confess. As if he'd become the center of gravity and there was no way she could resist that force.

Only one other person made her feel this way: Lucy Guardino. The thought brought with it a wave of resentment stronger than any invisible pull Oshiro wielded. "You have no right. Client confidentiality—"

"Only applies if you are a licensed private investigator. But seems like neither you nor Mr. Stone are licensed for anything..."

A loophole in the law she and Andre had taken advantage of: consultants didn't need to waste time or red tape with official licenses. "We get the job done. Our customers certainly don't complain— but they do expect that we respect their privacy."

His chin inclined a fraction—a very, very minute fraction—of an inch. "Of course. But public safety comes first. I'll have my men follow from a distance. As much for your partner's and Ms. Ames' protection as anything else."

If Oshiro saw Andre and Morgan leave for Monroeville, maybe Caine or one of his fellow escapees had as well? Damn it, she'd told Andre they should not have taken that job. "Did they see anyone?"

"No one else followed Mr. Stone and Ms. Ames."

That was good. Maybe she could use Morgan as bait to keep the marshals off Jenna's back while she collected Caine and the reward. "If you don't mind waiting until they finish our client consultation, I'll text Andre and tell him your men will be taking Morgan into protective custody."

Instead of relaxing, his lips tightened at her concession. As if he could see right through her ploy. Lucy would have if she'd been here. "Where is Lucy? She'll be at the top of Caine's list. Is she safe?"

"She is. Her daughter, as well."

"And Nick? Her husband?" Jenna had no clue how he put up with Lucy as his wife, probably the same reason why Nick was so good at his job—had counseled Andre, in fact. Occasionally, Jenna talked to him as well. Just with stuff she didn't want to dump on Andre.

"He insisted on staying in the city

until he could clear his patient schedule. But he's safe. Compared to you and Ms. Ames, he's at low risk. Perhaps we should talk about protective custody for you?"

"No. I'm fine. Clint's beef is with Lucy, not me." She cringed at the memory of how useless she'd been during that final confrontation with Clinton Caine.

"Clint?" Interest sparked his gaze. "Exactly how well do you know Caine?"

"Enough to know you shouldn't be wasting your time here with me. You should be out there trying to find him before he kills again."

Oshiro's stance was relaxed as he crossed his arms over his chest and waited. Standing in front of the door. Jenna ran through her repertoire of glares without luck. "You're not going to let me leave alone."

"I have no right to stop you. But doesn't mean you'll be going anywhere alone, no ma'am."

Jenna grabbed her gear and the map. Might not be a bad idea, having a few massively armed men at her beck and call. "Fine, then. But if we find anything,

Galloway and Stone get the credit." She flounced past him as he held the door open for her, then looked back over her shoulder. "And the reward."

CHAPTER 5

THE RADCLIFFE HOUSE surprised Morgan. When Andre drove them east on the Parkway out to Route 22, she'd been expecting to end up in one of the nouveau riche mini-mansions speckling the countryside beyond the Pittsburgh city limits. Instead, they'd arrived at a modest 1970's split-level in Monroeville.

No wonder Jenna hadn't wanted to come. Chasing after Clinton Caine promised fame and fortune—the return on investment in searching for a missing working class teenager could not compare. That's how Jenna measured everything:

did it help her get what she wanted? As long as you remained on the positive side of that equation, you remained in her life.

Sometimes Morgan could almost see the calculations spin through the air around Jenna when she was faced with a choice. It gave Morgan a clear advantage because it told her exactly how to manipulate Jenna, but lately she'd been surprised by how much Jenna's cold heart angered her. Not because she cared at all about Jenna, but because of Andre. He might be a tough, battle-scarred Marine, but his heart was as fragile as spun glass—and just as easily shattered.

Morgan knew that someday she might need to decide if Andre was better off without Jenna in his life. But for now, Jenna made Andre happy, so she let it rest.

"Thank goodness you came." A woman in her late thirties appeared at the front door, holding it open against the brisk March breeze. "Thank you," she said, nodding her head and bowing her shoulders to Andre as he passed by her into the house. She wore jeans and a cable knit sweater that was almost the same shade as her hair. Corn silk, the luke-cold color was probably named.

"Thank you," she repeated to Morgan, again with the strangely submissive head drop.

"Mrs. Radcliffe?" Andre asked as they crowded her slate-floored foyer that was maybe six feet square. Two sets of stairs led away from the tiny entryway: one headed up to an open floor plan with living room/dining room combo, kitchen, and hall presumably leading to bedrooms. The other led down to the garage and basement level. "I'm Andre Stone. From Galloway and Stone."

"Diane, call me Diane," their hostess said, her words pressured by nerves.

Andre and Morgan hung up their coats on the pegs she gestured to, alongside a crowded array of colorful knit hats and scarves and children's snow jackets. Diane touched Andre's arm as if reassuring herself that he was actually there and pointed the way to the living room, following him up the steps.

"This is my associate, Morgan

Ames," Andre made introductions once they'd all reached the landing at the top, another cramped area, this time carpeted. He side-stepped the entrance to the tiny galley kitchen to enter the living room, which featured a sectional sofa, its beige microsuede stained by a cocktail of fruit flavored colors, evidence of young children. A recliner took the place of honor in front of the bay window, directly across from a large flat screen TV and a wedding photo of Diane and a man wearing an Army dress uniform, his posture ramrod straight, his gaze bayonet sharp.

"Please, sit, sit," Diane Radcliffe said as she took a seat on the sofa then bounced back up again. "Oh wait, wait, I have it here, ready for you."

She bustled into the dining room, rummaged in a drawer of the faux-oak china cabinet, and returned holding a thick envelope. Still ignoring Morgan, she presented it to Andre and stepped back, dropping her head once again.

"I had to take a loan from my 401K," she said, directing her words to the carpet, "but I was able to get the ten thousand she asked for."

Finally she dared to look up, craning her neck to make eye contact with Andre, who towered over her. "It's all I have. But please, please, it has to be enough. Please find him. Find my boy and bring him home."

Morgan stepped back, leaving Andre and the mother in the center of the room. She knew what came next, and it wasn't her department.

Sure enough, the mother blubbered into tears, knees buckling. Right on cue, Andre caught her before she hit the floor and guided her to the sofa. She hugged his arm as sobs overwhelmed her, smearing his shoulder with snot.

Definitely not Morgan's department. She sidled into the galley-style kitchen—it was narrow, barely enough room for her to pass between the appliances and counters lining each side. As she rummaged through the cabinets until she found a glass, she noticed a magnet advertising Galloway and Stone affixed to the fridge, holding a coupon for a family portrait at the March Madness celebration at the mall. She hadn't realized Jenna had embarked on an advertising campaign—after their recent successes, they were turning away business. Typical Jenna, good was never good enough.

Morgan found a glass, filled it with water, grabbed a handful of napkins, and returned to set them on the glass and chrome coffee table in front of Andre and the woman. Newspapers from the last few days were scattered across the tabletop, including one folded to a story featuring Jenna and their last case. Guess it was obvious why Diane Radcliffe had thought to call them first when her son went missing.

While Morgan waited for the show of waterworks to end, she looked around. Family photos adorned the wall across from the large screen TV: a boy and girl, maybe eight to ten, both with their mother's washed-out blond hair, ran laughing and playing. A few formal family portraits with a frowning man—the soldier from the wedding photo, now looking awkward in his civilian clothing—

possessively circling his arms around the two kids and Diane; a third child, older, gangly with brown hair, standing outside the circle. That would be their subject, Gibson Radcliffe. Son of a previous relationship, saddled with the Radcliffe family name—although who the hell named their kid Gibson unless they had a death wish for the boy?—but never actually part of the Radcliffe family.

She counted nine framed photos: Gibson only appeared in the two formal portraits. Nowhere else. As if his parents—or his father, stepfather, whatever—wanted plausible deniability.

And now here they were. "Do you have a more recent photo?" she asked once the waterworks had subsided. Giving the parents something to do usually helped move things along.

Diane separated from Andre only far enough to reach first for the napkins to blow her nose and then for the envelope. She pushed it to Andre, even though it had been Morgan who requested the information. "It's all in there. Everything Mrs. Galloway asked for when I spoke with her on the phone."

Andre didn't bother to correct Diane's assumptions about Jenna's marital status as he turned the envelope upside down to empty its contents on the tabletop. He frowned at the cashier's check for the ten grand. Morgan knew he and "Mrs. Galloway" would be having a conversation about that, but personally, she approved of Jenna's tactic. It separated the serious clients from the ones who'd seen the news about Galloway and Stone and wanted to work with the best but pay nothing.

A few photos wafted out: a baby still in his hospital bassinette; a faded photo of a young, exhausted, but happy Diane cradling her newborn son; the requisite elementary school photo with a shy, toothy grin missing two teeth; a sullen pre-teen, lock of hair covering half his face, gaze missing the camera by a mile; and finally the downright belligerent, dead-eyed stare of a sixteen-year-old boy with a severe crew cut.

The life of Gibson Radcliffe played out like a poker hand. Not a winning one, either.

———•———

GIBSON MADE NOTE of the car's make and license plate. He took pictures of the black man and white girl who got out of it. The man, big and tall and dark, looked like some kind of comic book villain with his scars and scowl. All that vanished when Gibson's mom appeared, her face red from crying and worry. The big man treated her with tender regard, more sympathetic than the girl who came with him.

It was the girl he'd been waiting for.

She glanced over her shoulder, zeroing in almost exactly on Gibson's hiding spot. Her expression matched what Gibson saw every morning when he looked into the mirror. Before he put on his mask, his game face. It was getting harder and harder to find the energy to care enough about what anyone else thought to make the effort.

Now, thanks to his father, he didn't

need to bother any more. He was free. Free to be himself. To do what he wanted, when he wanted.

Free. To claim his birthright. To have fun.

CHAPTER 6

MORGAN STOOD ASIDE and let Andre handle the mother. It was obvious Diane Radcliffe had lived through some kind of long-term abuse—at the very least emotional abuse—and just as clear that she responded better to Andre. Maybe because he was former military, like her husband. Or maybe just because he was a man.

The way Diane only answered specific questions, never volunteered anything, and looked to Andre for both approval and permission with each answer, they were going to be here all day. The interview had to be completed, no doubt about that, but there was no reason for Morgan to stand here, bored to tears.

She wanted to get a move on; that way, she could convince Andre to divide and conquer. Any leads they got on Gibson's whereabouts she would use to leave Andre safely occupied while she continued the hunt for her father.

"Maybe I should search Gibson's room for clues?" she asked the mother, feeling stupid even using the word "clues." But the mother nodded as if this was exactly what she'd been expecting, hiring the famous—for Pittsburgh—firm of Galloway and Stone.

"Yes, of course. He has the downstairs."

Like there wasn't any symbolism in that, exiling the clearly unwanted and unloved problem child to the dungeon. Morgan fled down the steps, turned at the front door foyer, and continued down the second flight of stairs to the split-level's basement.

She turned the lights on and stood in

the doorway, surveying Gibson's kingdom
of gloom. There were blackout curtains on
the tiny basement windows perched high
along the front wall. The only light came
from an overhead fluorescent fixture,
accompanied by a subliminal whine that
made her teeth ache. The walls were
dark, fake wood paneling and the floor
linoleum in an orange and brown pattern.
Along the far side was a laundry area and
behind a flimsy accordion door a
bathroom with a shower stained with
mold. A rear door led out to the
backyard—she guessed it got a lot of use,
all the better to avoid mom and stepdad.

The entire space smelled of lemon-
scented fabric softener overwhelmed by
teenaged boy-funk. The saggy brown
tweed sofa bed had sheets poking out
between the cushions, but everything in
the room appeared centered around a
gaming chair on the floor in front of a TV
with a gaming console. A stack of generic
sodas stood within arm's reach of the
chair on one side with an open bag of
chips on the other.

Her phone rang before she could

begin to search for any more personal and pertinent details in the squalor. Micah.

"So," he said without preamble, "as sexy as it is, these late night chats and texting sessions, I've decided to do the right and honorable thing and ask you out on an official date."

She stared at the phone for a long moment, debating whether to hang up and pretend the call was dropped. Why did guys have such impeccable worst possible timing? Andre was the same way with Jenna, always trying to distract her with romantic gestures exactly when she needed to focus. Same with Nick and Lucy. She never understood why they put up with it.

Until now. Instead of ending the call, she said, "What if I'm not an honorable woman?"

Immediately she felt stupid with her pathetic attempt at banter. It wasn't her— not the real her. If need be, she could seduce any man to his knees...it was all an act, doing what she had to to get whatever Clint wanted. But that was all behind her. Now she was free to be herself. If she only had the faintest clue who or what that really was.

"Doesn't matter. Not to me. How's tonight work for you? I'm thinking I pick you up at seven, we'll go to dinner, maybe catch a movie after. Of course, that means you need to finally tell me where you live."

"Or I could meet you there," she countered as she opened the curtains, inviting a smudge of wan sunlight through the dirt-streaked basement windows. Micah wasn't stupid; he knew damn well she was no ordinary teenaged girl, but still he had this chivalrous side that insisted on seeing for himself that she wasn't caught in some dangerous living situation. Like having a depraved violent psychopath for a father...whoops, too late for that.

He didn't bother suppressing his sigh. "What is it? If we're never going to see each other in person, at least tell me why."

Anyone else, Morgan would have hung up and written them off as whiney, clingy Norms she was better off without.

But Micah wasn't whining. He was asking a perfectly reasonable, mature question and expected her to answer in the same fashion. With the truth.

"I'm at work now," she stalled. "I'll tell you everything. Next time I see you."

He didn't bother asking what kind of job—they'd first met while she was working undercover. "From your tone, I'm guessing that won't be tonight."

"No. But soon." Then she did something Morgan never, ever did. "I promise."

"You know you can't scare me off, right?" He made it sound like that was a good thing.

"That's exactly what I'm afraid of." She hung up before she could become entangled in any more lies or half-truths.

She tried very hard to only tell Micah the truth, parsed out in bite-sized bits that functioned as a smoke screen— and made her feel even more guilty than flat-out lying would have. Which said a lot about her feelings about him. Morgan had killed men without feeling a fraction of the regret and remorse that the thought of lying to Micah brought.

Only thing worse would be telling him the truth.

Alone in Gibson Radcliffe's dungeon of a room, Morgan shifted her focus back to the missing teenager. She began her search by looking for any indications of friends they could follow up with or places he might have gone by riffling through a desk cluttered with school notebooks and an old laptop that was virtually obsolete. As she scanned the computer's directories, she heard voices coming from the HVAC vent beside the desk.

"Why do you think Gibson may have left home?" It was Andre. He sounded frustrated, still trying to get a coherent answer from the mother. Morgan did not feel guilty at all about ditching him with the heavy lifting.

Diane stammered something Morgan couldn't hear. Andre tried again. "Why would he leave now? Did something happen? A trigger?"

"I was pregnant when I met my husband." Diane's voice sounded even more thin and reedy echoing through the ductwork than it had in person. "I never told Gibson who his real father was. But I think, maybe, he thinks..."

Morgan leaned closer to the grate, not sure if Diane trailed off or if for some reason she'd moved away from the upstairs vent. How many arguments about Gibson had her son listened to down here, she wondered. Bad enough to be exiled to this dank dungeon, but to have to listen to every unkind word your parents said about you? No wonder he'd left.

"You think he found out who his father is? That he's gone to meet him?" Andre asked.

"No. I don't see how he could have, not for certain. But I think, maybe, he's such an imaginative boy, no one ever sees that, they just see the outside, the problems..."

"What did Gibson think?" Andre persisted. "Who did he imagine was his real father?"

"He got this crazy notion. Became obsessed, even. With a man, a man he saw in the news..."

Morgan tensed. She suddenly had a

pretty good idea what Diane was going to say before she said it.

"I think, maybe, he went, he thought he could find him..."

"Find who, Mrs. Radcliffe?" Tension knotted Andre's voice and Morgan knew he'd come to the same conclusion as she had.

"Clinton Caine." The mother's words were punctuated with sobs. "The serial killer who just escaped from prison. Gibson thinks he's his father. God help me, I think he went to find him."

CHAPTER 7

To Jenna's surprise, Oshiro didn't argue about taking her car. Instead, he followed her to the building's parking garage and made her wait while he inspected her black Tahoe—the closest thing a civilian could come to a vehicle that was similar to what federal law enforcement used.

"Remote detonation isn't Clint's style," she told him as she watched in amusement while he ducked and rolled below the vehicle, shining his MagLite from front to back before standing once more. For such a bulky guy, he moved with the agility of a martial arts master.

"If he wanted to kill me, he'd do it up close and personal."

"If you were the target," Oshiro said, popping the hood and inspecting the engine compartment. "But if he were trying to flush out his daughter—"

Jenna blinked. She'd imagined herself the hunter stalking Caine. She did not like the idea of being cannon fodder in the psychopathic games he and Morgan engaged in.

Oshiro slammed the hood shut. "All clear." He said a few more words into his phone, alerting his men that they were ready to move.

Jenna almost changed her mind, ready to slam the door on both Clinton Caine and his daughter once and for all, but she couldn't shut out the memories of when Caine held her captive. She'd been bait then as well—he wasn't interested in her, wanted only Lucy Guardino, the FBI agent who'd put a stop to his original killing spree—but knowing that hadn't made it any less terrifying.

She never wanted to feel that helpless again. Just as she never wanted to feel like she did now: a rabbit caught in a trap, powerless to run or hide, doomed to simply wait for the predator to decide to finish things once and for all. No. This ended. Now.

Resolve fortified, she strode forward and held her hand out to Oshiro for her car keys. His lips quirked in that weird half-smile of his—she had no idea if it was amusement, disdain, puzzlement, or annoyance—but he dropped the keys into her palm without argument.

She stashed her gear in the back and got into the driver's seat, feeling more in control. Oshiro climbed into the passenger's seat. Wordlessly, she handed him the map and pointed to the nearest location Morgan had circled, a remote crossroads about twenty miles out of town, up in the mountains past Slickville. "We'll try there first."

He radioed their destination to his men and instructed two of them to remain to watch the premises. "Any idea what's waiting for us?" he asked as she drove them out of the garage and turned onto Braddock.

"Nope. Morgan said it was a money cache, that's all."

He scrutinized the map then switched to his phone. "Not much around there. Farmland, a junkyard, a few buildings at the crossroad. Not even a proper town. Could be anything. A bag of cash buried under a rock. Or hidden down an old well or mine shaft."

"Maybe he buried it under a pigsty." She liked the thought of watching Oshiro and his fellow deputy marshals shovel shit.

"Maybe. But I doubt Caine likes to get his hands dirty—at least not that way. Other than the actual killings, in most of his crimes, he used proxies."

"His children, you mean." It was Caine's twisted idea of family: he'd raised his children to steal for him so he wouldn't have to worry about making a living, taught them to lure innocent women into his hands, even groomed one of them—Morgan—into joining in on his killing sprees. "Why haven't you come after Morgan before?"

"Not my job. She was never arrested

or charged with anything so wasn't on my radar until Caine escaped and we learned she was a person of interest."

He shifted in his seat. "You were still a federal agent when you and Lucy Guardino caught Caine. But there's not a whole lot in your report about Morgan. Only her name and a vague description. There's no official records on her, no prints, no clear photos. Just a blurry video—we think she was there when that sheriff's deputy, William Bob, was killed. Whether she was a victim, witness, or suspect, why didn't you and Guardino go after her?"

Deputy Bob. Jenna had liked him. Not pursuing Morgan for his death was one of the reasons why she'd stopped working with Lucy Guardino. She'd never forgive Lucy for letting Morgan get away with that murder—and who knew how many others. Lucy had had more important things on her mind at the time, like saving Jenna and several children, and they had no actual evidence against Morgan, but still... "I wish I knew. It was Lucy's call. Not mine."

Oshiro made a small noise between a grunt and a sigh. Acknowledging Jenna's shirking of her responsibility? Or agitation at Lucy's betrayal of everything a law enforcement officer was sworn to uphold and protect? She wished she knew—it would help her decide how much she could trust him.

But Oshiro did not enlighten her. Instead, he swiveled his head to check their mirrors for any signs of pursuit. Then he glanced back at the map again. "What are these numbers to the side of the GPS coordinates? Some kind of address? Rural route maybe?"

"Morgan wrote those. Not sure what they mean. Guess we'll find out when we get there." This time of day, traffic was light. Until they turned onto Route 22 and began to hit all the red lights through Murrysville.

"Tell me about Morgan," Oshiro continued. "Why did you decide to work with her? I mean, if you believe she really is the daughter of a serial killer."

As if it had actually been Jenna's choice. "Like you said, she's not currently wanted for any crime." Not even Deputy Bob's murder, which was still on the books as an open case. The video had shown Morgan in the building but not the actual crime... In fact, if all you saw was the recording, she appeared to be a hostage or possible victim. Anything but the killer Jenna knew her to be.

"But you know what she's capable of." He must have done his homework, seen the video, judged Morgan for himself. Or was it Jenna he was judging?

Jenna knew better than anyone what Morgan was capable of. But Morgan also knew Jenna's secrets—had evidence of Jenna killing two gangbangers who'd set up an ambush, ready to kill her or any other law enforcement officer who came their way. Jenna had been alone, without backup, on her way to save Lucy and several civilians from more violent gangbangers during the Homewood riots last Christmas, and she hadn't had time to follow procedure.

Instead, she'd killed the men in cold blood without ever giving them a chance to surrender or even raise their weapons.

Technically, that made her just as guilty as Morgan—a fact Morgan hadn't hesitated to capitalize on when she came to Jenna looking for a job.

"I know Morgan is a stone-cold killer at heart. I also know that she's risked her own life to save mine and Andre's and dozens of civilians. More than once."

"Those school kids she helped save from the fire." He really had done his homework.

"And more lives saved during the Homewood riots. Lucy can verify that for you." A good chunk of the city had burned down during that night of violence, and Morgan had no reason to be there. She could have waited safely on the sidelines, not gotten involved. But she'd gone to save Lucy—who, as usual, didn't need saving—and had instead almost died saving Jenna. More leverage she held over Jenna. Somehow the scales were always tipped in Morgan's favor.

Maybe now was Jenna's chance to find a way to deal with both Morgan and her father once and for all. Gain some leverage of her own.

"So, you trust her?" Oshiro asked.

Trust? Morgan? The two words did not even belong in the same universe. "No. I don't trust her. But I can rely on her for one thing: to always do whatever is in her best interest. Right now, that means playing the good girl, pretending to be a hero, saving lives."

She couldn't keep the contempt from her tone and Oshiro picked up on it. "You think she's like her father. A psychopath."

"No. I think she's worse. There's a reason why Clinton Caine lived underground all those years—he couldn't maintain a mask of normalcy long enough to survive out in the open. But Morgan, she's a chameleon. If they gave Oscars for psychopathic performances, she'd win every category. Normal people like her, they let her inside their guard. That makes her much more dangerous than Clint."

"Because they want to trust her," Oshiro mused. "That's the key to any undercover work. Manipulate the responses of the people around you until they're totally invested in believing whatever you have to sell them."

Maybe the deputy marshal was smarter than he looked. They passed through Delmont and started up Route 819.

"Are you going to arrest her? You have men watching her and Andre, right?"

"Nothing to arrest her for—like you said, there's nothing to charge her with. But take her in for an interview? Oh yes. Definitely."

Which meant Jenna had to hope that Morgan didn't see being picked up by the feds as a threat. Otherwise she might play her ace in the hole, and it might be Jenna arrested for murder.

CHAPTER 8

GIBSON RADCLIFFE THOUGHT he was Clinton Caine's son? Morgan sincerely doubted it was true—Clint kept close tabs on all his offspring and had never mentioned Gibson. More likely Gibson was just another lost kid hanging onto a delusion he hoped would turn him from a no one into a someone.

She wondered when Gibson's obsession with Clint had begun. A quick search of Gibson's computer revealed a folder labeled "Trig" that actually contained clippings of Clint's crimes and his capture. There were a lot of them—

Clint's depravity and his willingness to speak to the press made sure he'd grabbed headlines across the country.

She also found drafts of letters from Gibson to Clint. The kid was definitely a fan, that was for certain. Talked about proving himself worthy of Clint, making him proud...poor kid had no clue that Clint received dozens of letters like his every day.

In prison, Clint wouldn't have had access to email, so Gibson must have sent paper letters—and if Clint replied, it would have also been via regular postal mail. She continued to ransack the books and other papers strewn around Gibson's lair. Nothing from the prison. She debated calling Jenna to see if any of her former Postal Service connections might be able to track any correspondence but decided against it. The feds would have already checked that.

Besides, Clint was much too smart to ever put anything on paper that could be used against him. The most he would have done was to arrange future, more secure communications. Maybe using his lawyer as a conduit...but only if he had use for the boy.

As she continued her search, she wondered at that. Clint and the other two prisoners would have needed help to coordinate their escape. Transportation, clothes, food, shelter, cash, weapons... They had to have had an outside accomplice, and who better than a malleable teenager desperate for a father figure? Gibson certainly fit the bill.

Which meant it was no coincidence Gibson's mother had called on Galloway and Stone to investigate his disappearance. She'd bet it was Gibson who placed that magnet so prominently on the family refrigerator and who made certain his mother saw the article that featured Jenna and Andre.

Big question was: how well did Gibson cover his tracks? He would have left an obvious trail for Morgan to follow— one that led to where Clint wanted Morgan to go, no doubt a trap.

She took another look at the ancient laptop. Nothing. He'd cleared all of his accounts, the only thing remaining an automatic reminder about a family portrait appointment at the mall tonight. She was surprised Gibson still cared enough to join in on the ritual—not as if many of his photos made the wall of honor upstairs.

She kept looking, digging deeper into the computer's files. No way could a sixteen-year-old kid from Monroeville hide all evidence of the logistics needed to assist a prison break. Maybe he had another computer he'd taken with him? Or maybe he'd used his phone for everything?

No. Clint distrusted phones, he would have minimalized any communication using them. She scanned the room once more. It was obvious that the most-used piece of furniture was the gaming chair. She sat down in it, ignoring the reek of testosterone-laden sweat that emanated from it, and reached for Gibson's controller. Computer games—the one piece of modern technology Clinton Caine had embraced.

Especially after he discovered their dual function as communication devices—

communication many adults were oblivious to. Before he was arrested, Clint had established a multitude of gaming aliases and used them to engage his "boys," as he called the collected group of offspring spawned via his rampage of rapes and abductions.

As Morgan scrolled through the games and retraced Gibson's latest virtual steps, she shook her head at the irony. Of all his children, Clint had only truly been interested in the males, hoping to find a protégé worthy of continuing his bloody legacy. It had been Morgan, his eldest daughter, who had filled that role...and yet, even now, he was still focused on grooming a boy, not even his own blood, to be his partner in crime.

Or maybe he was preparing Gibson as a Judas goat? Setting him up to take the fall? Typical Clint, he'd have a dozen scenarios mapped out, all of them ensuring that Clint escaped and someone else paid the price. She almost felt sorry for Gibson.

Part of the gaming system was the ability to swap points earned in virtual reality for gift cards that could be used as real world cash to purchase merchandise. Once she cracked Gibson's account, it was easy to trace the ebb and flow of points and cash gifted to him by various online sponsors—all of whom would eventually be traced back to Clint or the other two prisoners, no doubt.

She envisioned Clint sitting in his cell, his fingers flying over a handheld gaming console small enough to be smuggled in and hidden from the guards, weaving his web of deception around lonely, desperate Gibson.

Gibson was a good choice. Pliable enough that he'd obeyed Clint—as evidenced by the purchases of freeze-dried food, enough for several men for several weeks, a dozen prepaid calling cards and burner cells, a variety of knives and hunting equipment, oh, and look there, a nice stockpile of ammo and handguns. Now, if she could just discover where all of this treasure trove was sent...but Gibson wasn't that dumb. He'd most likely completed the transactions using a burner phone. Untraceable.

She went back to Gibson's gaming history, tried to see if he'd created any other accounts tied to his real life activities. Wait. An account in his stepfather's name—created two years ago but unused until last month. Then it was reactivated and used to buy several kilos of sodium metal, phosphorus, camping fuel tablets, two dozen large canisters of gel fuel, and remote car starters.

Each alone was fairly unremarkable. Put them all together and...

"How's it going down here?" Andre's voice interrupted her thoughts. He stood in the doorway, holding Diane's precious envelope of memories. "Any luck?"

"None of it good." She didn't mention Gibson's communications with Clint—for right now, those were for her eyes only. But this new information made for an excellent diversion to occupy Andre's time. She showed him the purchases made in Gibson's stepfather's name. "I have a feeling Gibson isn't working on a project for the school science fair."

Andre squinted at the screen

displaying the list, his forehead knotting. "Our lost boy is planning to blow something up."

"Not only blow it up—also burn it down," she corrected. "He's got the makings for several wicked incendiary devices. Enough to—"

"Bring down a good sized building. His school?"

Diane Radcliffe came into the room. Somehow she seemed even smaller and more mouse like here in her son's domain.

"Any luck?" she asked eagerly.

"We found a few indications of intent," Andre said, obviously stalling as he gestured for Morgan to turn off the TV.

"Intent?" She echoed the word, her tone puzzled.

"Gibson wanted to leave. He had a plan. And he covered his tracks."

Diane shook her head, her gaze darting around the room as if expecting her son to pop out of the woodwork and tell her this was all a joke. "I don't understand. Why would a sixteen-year-old boy plan to simply vanish? Leave everything, his family, his life behind? It makes no sense."

Sure it did. But Morgan said nothing, let Andre do the heavy lifting. The mother responded better to him anyway.

Andre continued, "You told me Gibson was having trouble with some of the kids at school. Is there any chance that he might want to get even? That he might be planning something?"

"No. No. He's not like that. He'd never hurt anyone."

"I'm sorry, we have to ask."

"No. That's impossible." Her tone grew strident and for the first time she raised her face to meet Andre's gaze. "Why would you even think that?"

Because he fits the profile of a mass murderer, Morgan thought. Even before he hooked up with a psychopathic serial killer as a mentor and father figure. But she kept her mouth shut. She was more interested in the SUV idling at the curb. A black Tahoe. Exactly like the feds used. More than surveilling if they parked directly in front of the house—a very weak tactical position unless you wanted to make sure whoever was inside the house knew you were coming.

Which meant they weren't here for Gibson or his psychokiller mad bomber plans. They were here for her.

CHAPTER 9

JENNA FOLLOWED OSHIRO'S directions to the site of Clinton Caine's money cache. They followed the switchbacks of a county road over a mountain then into a valley that appeared virtually uninhabited except for one lone farmhouse in the far distance and a few buildings clustered together about a mile ahead. Fields plowed for the spring planting spread out on both sides of the road, leaving them no cover for their approach.

She pulled the Tahoe to the gravel shoulder. "That's the place?"

"That's the place," he confirmed,

nodding to the crossroads ahead. A second black Tahoe pulled in behind them. Oshiro's partner, a slim black woman with her hair pulled back in cornrows, waited at the wheel.

Jenna and Oshiro got out. Jenna opened the rear hatch and pulled out a monocular while Oshiro one-upped her by retrieving a pair of thermal imaging binoculars from his own vehicle. She climbed up to the roof of her SUV and scouted ahead.

"There are a few trailers, two buildings—one looks like an old service station, the other I'm not sure—and a Quonset hanger with a bunch of vehicles scattered around it. Maybe a junkyard."

"Or chop shop," he suggested, handing her the thermal binocs. "This should give you a better idea of what we're dealing with."

She scanned the buildings once more. This time she could see the heat signatures of several people. "Looks like four or five in the hanger, two in the first trailer, one in the second, and..." She focused on the brick building beside the service station. It was cube-shaped but with a high pitched roof—some kind of church? It had a solid feel to it, as if it had been there much longer than any of the other structures. Whatever it was, there was a lot of activity going on inside. "I count at least eleven in the second building—hard to say, they keep moving, and there are several blind spots."

"The only people we've seen in the past ten miles and they're all right here where Clinton Caine stashed his cash?"

"Clint isn't exactly the social type." Jenna accepted his hand as she climbed down from the Tahoe's roof. "Maybe the stash is nearby? The crossroads are simply a landmark?"

He squinted at his phone, zooming in. "Morgan's coordinates would be directly over that second building. The brick one with all the people in it." He glanced around, assessing their approach. "Maybe they know something. Can't hurt to ask."

"They'll see us coming, know exactly who we are." Well, at least Oshiro—no mistaking him for anything except law enforcement.

"We're not hiding anything. Let's see if they are."

"If you go in and Clint's there, you'll scare him off."

"And you won't? He knows your face."

"He won't run. He's not scared of me." Exactly the opposite. Caine saw her as one of his victims, his "fish," he called them. "I'll go in alone."

Oshiro's frown tightened his face into a fearsome scowl. "No. I don't like it. Not until we see who's in there."

"We don't have time to wait for backup." She reached into the Tahoe for her ankle holster and strapped it on, then pulled her pants leg down over it. Clint would know she was armed, but he wouldn't care—it would probably make him laugh. "Besides, what are the odds that he's even there? He's been free for four days now, has most likely already been and gone. It's info we're after, not an arrest or capture."

He strode back to the other vehicle, handed the binoculars to his partner, and spoke to her for several moments before returning to Jenna's Tahoe. "Lester is going to hang back, cover the perimeter for us. Just in case."

"Lester?"

"Monica Lester. Sorry, should have introduced you."

"Not so much concerned about the social niceties as I am one woman covering our backs."

He grinned. "You haven't met Lester. Don't worry, she's up to it."

They climbed back into the Tahoe and drove toward the crossroads. Jenna glanced in the rearview mirror as the SUV following them peeled off, heading cross-country to a small knoll in the center of the field, the only high ground available. "She's a sniper?"

"One of the best." He glanced out his window, following the trail of dust Lester's SUV left in its wake. "That will place her at an angle where she can cover most of the pie—we'll need to worry about the blind slice between the rear of the building and the gas station." He waved his hand, indicating an area from around ten o'clock to eleven.

They reached the intersection. Jenna came to a stop, even though there was no stop sign in either direction. The peaked roof brick building dominated the landscape. Up close, she made out brass letters across the soffit above the entrance: Crossroads.

"What do you think it is?" she asked Oshiro. "A church?" Wouldn't it be just like Clint to hide his ill-gotten gains in a house of worship?

Oshiro shrugged, too busy using his mirrors to scout their surroundings one final time. "You'll want to park there, gives us cover if we need to make a strategic retreat."

Jenna pulled the Tahoe around to park it face out where he indicated, a spot diagonally in front of the brick building, where they'd be in Lester's sights. "You know we did have tactical training in the Postal Service."

"Only reason why you're here. Not that it matters, you're staying in the vehicle."

"Like hell I am."

He squinted at her over the top of his sunglasses. "I could arrest you. Accessory. Material witness."

"Good try, but we don't have any proof that the information I gave you has anything to do with Clinton Caine, not until we go inside. Besides, it came from Morgan, not me."

She was expecting an argument— Lucy would have argued, then ignored whatever Jenna told her and done things her own damn way. In truth, Jenna teetered on the knife-edge between adrenaline and fear, and she secretly hoped for a reason to stay behind.

Oshiro merely pushed his sunglasses back up his nose with one knuckle, hiding both his eyes and any hint of expression on his face, before finally nodding his acceptance. He couldn't get rid of her, the twist of his lips suggested, so he might as well make use of her. "Guess that means you go in first. After I scout around back and see what we're dealing with."

"I'm not an idiot. But I'm also not about to be a sitting duck. You realize they have eyes on us right now."

He glanced out the window and adjusted his side mirror. "Not just from our target building. Across the street, as well." He nodded to the Quonset hut that filled his mirror. "Guess we do it your way. We'll go in together. You do the talking, I'll do the shooting."

He was joking. At least Jenna hoped he was. But the way his face was set, all expression erased, it would have been easier to read a stone.

CHAPTER 10

MORGAN THOUGHT ABOUT running. But what good would that do her except land her firmly on law enforcement's radar? Something she'd worked very hard to avoid. She quickly ran an inventory. Barrettes with their handcuff shims, no way the cops would notice those or her sunglasses. Decoy wallet with her fake ID was in her coat pocket hanging in the foyer. She had her knives—nothing illegal there, so she wasn't worried—but her pistol with the serial numbers removed would need to be left behind.

As Andre revealed the damning

evidence found in Gibson's game console, Morgan sat down, slid the pistol from her boot, and nudged it under the sleeper sofa. Given the dust bunnies rustling in the wake of her swift movement, it was safe there, especially as she doubted that Diane ever let her younger kids down here in Gibson's territory. The cops would find it, think it was part of Gibson's stash.

"You're wrong," Diane kept repeating. "You must be wrong."

Time to end this. Morgan stood and joined Andre and the distraught mother. "I'm sorry, Mrs. Radcliffe, but we need to tell the authorities."

"What? No, you can't. What will my husband say? And you can't prove Gibson has done anything wrong."

"Actually, ma'am, we can. I'm afraid your son also assisted Clinton Caine in his prison break. Federal agents are outside. They're going to need this gaming console and access to Gibson's computer and other belongings." It was her ace in the hole and she hated to give it up, but the feds could trace Gibson's online activity faster than she could. Besides, wherever he'd had them delivered, she could guarantee it was nowhere close to where Clint was now. Gibson was merely the marionette—Clint was pulling his strings, and Clint was no dummy.

Andre glanced at her, startled. Morgan took over the game controller and scrolled back to the messages she'd tied to Clint. He frowned. "She's right, Diane. We can't wait any longer."

"We'll get you through this, Mrs. Radcliffe. All part of the Galloway Stone service." Morgan sweetened her performance by wrapping an arm around Diane and helping her to the sofa. "Mr. Stone, should we invite the agents inside?"

Andre creased his brow at her but followed her glance out the window and nodded. Together they went upstairs to the foyer.

"They're here for me," she whispered before he could open the front door. "But I can't help them, not as much as the info we've found on Gibson can."

It only took him a moment to put everything together. "It was no coincidence Diane called us. Your father planned all this. But why? What good does it do him if you're picked up by the police?"

"It wasn't Clint. I think it was Gibson himself. He knows who I am, and he wants to send me a message—that he's better than me, that he's the one Clint should be working with. He's trying to prove himself a worthy partner."

He glanced back down the stairs to the basement where they'd left Diane. "She didn't even ask when we'd called the police."

"I don't think she's the type who questions much of anything in her life." It sounded harsher than she'd intended. She softened her tone for Andre's benefit more than Diane's. "I get the feeling she's never had that luxury."

He gave a slow nod and returned his attention back to Morgan. "I hope you're not thinking of going out the back, because I can't cover for you."

"No. Wouldn't do me any good in the long run, anyway." Not because she intended to stay with the cops, but because she needed time to see what they knew about Clint. "You know they won't want to let me go, right?"

"Might not be a bad thing. Couple of days stashed away in a safe house."

"You more worried about keeping me safe or keeping me out of trouble?"

To anyone else, his expression would have been unreadable through the scars that lined his face. But she saw the smile flit across his lips. "Both." Then he glanced at her. "You worried about something else?"

They both knew she was too smart and too careful to have ever left anything easily incriminating at a crime scene—not even her fingerprints. "Not about anything they'd find today. But I don't like being bagged and tagged like some sort of wild animal, a trail of digital footprints waiting to catch up to me someday."

"They don't have anything to arrest you for. Not like you've been helping Caine." God bless him. Jenna would have twisted the last into a sneer and a question, while Andre stated it as fact.

"The only way they could have known I was here was if Jenna sent them. What if she told them I helped her by giving her the locations of two of Clint's stashes? If she finds anything there and tells the cops, then I'm an accessory. If she doesn't and tells the cops, then I'm obstructing justice."

"Jenna wouldn't do that." A trace of doubt tainted his words. They both knew if it suited Jenna's purposes, she'd betray Morgan without blinking twice. "She needs you," he added, his tone firm, back on solid ground. "What good would it do her to have you taken into custody?"

Leverage, Morgan thought. Not to mention the ability to use Morgan's fingerprints against her in the future, if they were recorded in a federal database. Jenna was smart, she knew how to build an air-tight frame-up if she ever decided Morgan was a liability. Morgan didn't hold it against Jenna—it was exactly what Morgan would do if their roles were reversed.

"It won't come to that," Andre filled the silence. "Just tell them what you can to help them find Caine, then you won't have anything to worry about."

"Except our friendly neighborhood mad bomber on the loose." One good thing about the cops showing up at Gibson's house, he was now their headache.

"That was smart, the way you found those messages in the video game."

"I'm not just another pretty face."

He smiled and she mirrored it. Not because she was playing him, but because Andre's smiles were always genuine and well earned.

"Absolutely not. Did you see anything in there that might tell us what his target is or when?"

"Didn't have enough time. Which is why you need to make a deal with the cops. The info we have on Gibson in exchange for them letting you stay on the case, helping them find Gibson and whatever he has planned for those IEDs. After all, it's what we were hired to do." And an excellent way for Andre to stay out of Clint's sights and safely within range of well-armed law enforcement types.

He frowned, obviously suspicious of her motives, but opened the door and strode outside to greet the cops.

Morgan took the opportunity to riffle through her coat pockets and lift her wallet with the fake ID. The one thing that could get her arrested. The cops would be searching the house, looking for evidence against Gibson. She eyed the younger kids' winter coats and hats. No, it was supposed to snow tonight and tomorrow; they'd find it too soon.

"Can I get you a glass of water, Mrs. Radcliffe?" she called down the stairs, even as she was dashing for the kitchen. With the water running, she turned the disposal on and slid the fake driver's license down it. A few seconds later, bye-bye Devon Wilson, age twenty-two, address in Shadyside.

As she ran back down to the basement with a glass of water, she glanced out the front window. Andre was talking to one man, the other was on his cell. Calling for backup, no doubt. Maybe it was better this way. It meant Andre would be safe, working with the cops. The cops would be busy ransacking Gibson's life. And she'd get a look at the manhunt's operation firsthand, maybe get an idea where to look for Clint. Or where not to.

She sat next to Diane and placed the water on the table. The mother was too shaky to trust with anything she could break or spill. Diane turned to her, her face splotchy with tears. "I don't understand any of this. What was Gibson thinking?"

Morgan didn't really care too much about Gibson's plans. She was more concerned about how those plans intersected with Clint's. No way in hell would Clint partner with an amateur like Gibson without having an ulterior motive. Whatever target Gibson was planning to bomb would almost certainly be some kind of smokescreen for Clint.

Clint had already escaped custody, why would he risk being caught during some mass killing spectacle? What game was he playing?

CHAPTER 11

AFTER SHOWING THE two federal agents how to access the messages on the gaming console, Morgan left Andre behind with the still weeping Diane and climbed into the back seat of a patrol car that the agents had summoned to escort her to the command post coordinating the local search for Clint and his fellow escapees.

The two police officers looked at her with curiosity but said nothing—obviously they'd been instructed not to ask questions and simply to deliver her into the hands of the fugitive task force. They didn't have far to go. The task force had taken over the offices of a defunct travel agency in a small strip mall on Route 22.

Morgan knew from the news that the State Troopers were running the show, with assistance from the FBI, US Marshals, and a variety of local law enforcement agencies. Made sense, Clint and the other escapees were in state custody at the time they'd escaped.

The cops had established several command posts extending in a radius from the State Police barracks in Ebensburg, near where the fugitives had last been sighted, expanding outward to areas of interest. In Clint's case, that meant following his old trucking routes extending from Huntington past Pittsburgh, giving the task force a wide area—wilderness, farmland, suburbs, small towns, and the city—to cover.

The travel agency was on the first floor of a two-story whitewashed concrete building. Part of the top floor was being renovated—a bright yellow construction debris chute caught Morgan's eye as it led down from a second floor window into a dumpster parked in the alley between the building and its Chinese take-out restaurant neighbor. The other part of the top floor was occupied by a lawyer specializing in accident claims, an 800 number emblazoned across his windows.

There was no special security as the officers walked Morgan through the front door of the former travel agency. No lobby, no metal detectors, no one manning the reception desk—just a cubicle farm filled with weary law enforcement professionals, most with phones to their ears while also working at computers.

Several large maps littered with notations were duct-taped to a wall—they appeared wrinkled and worn, as if they'd been taken down from other temporary locations before finding their way here. Which was probably the truth since, as the search area expanded, the command posts would have moved as well. There was none of the Hollywood glamor that the public at large associated with a manhunt.

Some of the task force members looked up from their work to stare at

Morgan with disdain and contempt, others with a hint of fear, many with frank curiosity as if she were a freak in a circus sideshow. Whatever stories Jenna had told them, they appeared to be having difficulty reconciling them with the polite, pretty young woman in the pink coat.

When her escorts stopped to talk to one of the officers manning a desk at the front of the room, Morgan drifted past the cubicles in a seemingly aimless pattern that was anything but as she zeroed in on the maps with their search grids and notations. No matter that she was here, in the lion's den, and could be arrested herself at any moment. She wasn't nervous or afraid. She was hunting her prey—something she shared with these men and women. Only difference was she was going to find him while, despite their superior numbers and technology, they didn't stand a chance in hell.

She casually leaned against one of the empty cubicles as she continued her reconnaissance. Although the officers had their own laptops and cell phones, each cubicle also had its own landline. It was obvious these guys weren't fielding random tips from a hotline, so any communications they received would be high-value intel.

She glanced around. No one watching the brunette civilian in the pink coat. It would only take a minute for her to program the phones to forward to hers, allowing her to listen in to any incoming calls. She kept her posture relaxed, bored even, as she reached behind her and eased the phone's handset off its cradle and punched in the numbers. Twenty-two seconds later it was done.

"This is her?" a woman's voice cut through the din.

Morgan spun around, her most gracious smile plastered to her face. A petite African-American woman had emerged from the back hallway and was staring at her. Like the other officers, the woman was dressed for field work in utilitarian cargo pants, a gray polo shirt, and windbreaker with the state police logo on it.

It was clear from the way the others glanced up at the sound of her voice that she was in charge. It was equally clear from the woman's clear, no bullshit gaze as she visually dissected Morgan that she was not going to be an easy mark. Good thing Morgan enjoyed a challenge.

"Corporal Liz Harding." The woman didn't extend her hand as she introduced herself. Morgan had the feeling it wasn't meant as a slight, rather simply a reflection of how many things the State Trooper was juggling right now, day four of the search for three killer fugitives. Manners meant time wasted. Morgan liked that.

"How can I help, Corporal?" She followed Harding to her cubicle at the edge of the maze closest to the wall with the map. Since she still wore her pink wool coat and other young professional accouterments, Morgan decided to stick with that persona. Seemingly helpful while actually on a reconnaissance mission. By the time she left, she'd know exactly where *not* to waste her time searching for Clint as well as what leads the task force was following.

"Call me Liz," Harding said absently,

her focus on a sheaf of papers, folders, and maps strewn across a cubicle desk. Morgan took the seat beside her.

Even better than her coup with the landline would be a chance to clone Harding's cell phone, but that would take longer and physical access to the cell, and she didn't see someone as guarded as Harding leaving her phone unattended. Morgan slid her own phone into her hand concealed within her coat pocket as she considered her options. Maybe she could do something with the laptop? A RAT attack? The remote access Trojan horse would allow her to gain control of the microphone so she could listen in, plant a keystroke logger, and access admin privileged info. She had the software, but she needed the opportunity to use it without interruption.

She forced herself to remain patient and instead focused on the map taped to the wall behind Harding. The cops were building a geographic profile of each of the escapees, but it was obvious they had much more data for Clint than any of the others. Made sense since Western

Pennsylvania had been his stalking ground for almost two decades. In fact, a geographic profile was how Lucy had discovered him originally.

Morgan made note of the areas they'd already searched and cleared as well as the presumptive sightings. Not all of the sightings would be true ones, but since she knew Clint and his habits intimately, she could eliminate potential false leads far more easily than the cops could.

As she stared at the map, she was both frustrated and relieved. Frustrated because there was no discernable pattern—and there should have been. Clint was a creature of habit. Relieved because if the cops weren't close to finding him, she still had a chance to get to him first. Clint behind bars was almost as dangerous as Clint on the loose, so the best solution for everyone, especially Morgan, was Clint dead and buried.

"Can I see some ID?" Harding asked, interrupting Morgan's fantasies of exactly how she'd end Clint. Her favorite would be to use her well-honed CQC knife. Ironic, since it had been Clint who taught her how to wield a blade with surgical precision.

"Sorry, didn't know I'd need any." Morgan kept her voice relaxed.

Harding's glance was sharp-edged. "I have conflicting reports on your age, Ms. Ames. Do we need to notify a parent or guardian? There's nothing in the database to verify your identity. "

Something Morgan prided herself on, but it obviously made the state trooper uncomfortable. Then Harding flipped open one of the manila files. To a blurred shot of Morgan leaving the scene of Deputy Bob's murder.

The cubicle suddenly felt small and intimate, almost as intimate as killing Bob had been. Morgan felt distanced from the person she'd been back then. It didn't feel like her, not at all. The girl who'd killed the deputy had been totally in Clint's thrall, unable to think or act for herself. If she hadn't killed Bob, Clint would have killed her. Simple self-defense. Only the law would never see it that way.

Nor would they understand what it truly was: survival of the fittest. Bob had been fooled by Morgan's youthful appearance, thought she was a lost little girl who needed his help. Morgan glanced from the photo to Harding and saw that the state trooper would not be similarly taken in.

"Is this you?" Harding asked, tapping the photo of the pony-tailed little girl dressed in a bulky snow coat and puffy hat. The girl could have been half Morgan's age, and other than the same dark hair and eyes, there was little resemblance to how Morgan looked now.

Morgan shook her head, not committing anything to the record. She assumed they were being recorded, even if they weren't, it was always best to think and act that way. "I'm not sure how I can help, Corporal Harding."

"You can start by cutting the bullshit," Harding said without raising her voice. She didn't need to, given that their chairs were mere inches apart.

The fabric-covered cardboard that created the cubicle's walls gave a false sense of privacy. Despite the fact that Harding hadn't raised the volume of her voice, her tone had cut through the conversations surrounding them and Morgan felt the focus of all of the law enforcement officers in the room suddenly on her.

"You are not under arrest," Harding continued. "Not yet. Give me a reason—" She stopped herself, her gaze on Morgan's face, obviously realizing threats were not the way to get what she wanted. "Give me a reason to believe you," she pivoted, "and we can bring in Clinton Caine. Together. Something we both want, correct?"

"Correct." Morgan liked Harding. She was a lot like Andre, except not as warm and fuzzy—no, wait, not Andre, Harding reminded Morgan of a less-seasoned, younger version of Lucy Guardino. "Jenna Galloway didn't send you to get me, did she?"

Harding hesitated, deciding on her play, then led with the truth. "We followed you from her office. We've been surveilling Galloway and Stone for three days now."

"On the advice of Lucy Guardino."
Morgan wasn't asking a question, but
Harding answered with a slight nod
before she caught herself. Now things
were making more sense. Lucy might not
be here in person, but it was clear she
was directing the manhunt from afar.
Keeping her family safe—both by staying
away and by staying involved. A balancing
act only Lucy could pull off.

Morgan leaned forward and grabbed
a pen from the caddy beside the phone.
"Okay, then. Let's start with this map."
She began to circle areas of potential
usefulness—bolt-holes Clint might turn to
if Gibson hadn't been able to provide an
adequate hiding place for him and his
comrades...if the escapees were even still
together. Clint would go off on his own as
soon as the others lost their usefulness,
but that was assuming Clint was the one
in charge.

The balance of power in a small
group could influence so many things:
how fast they moved, how they divided
themselves, if they hid out or tried to put

more distance between themselves and the authorities... Morgan hesitated, her pen hovering over the map. How would Lucy approach the problem?

"Tell me about the others," she asked Harding. "The men who escaped with Clint."

"Dead-eyed killers, each of them," Harding answered. "Brothers, Pete and Paul Kroft, serving life for a spree of home invasions that left seven dead, including an eighty-two-year-old great-grandmother, who they raped and burned alive."

Morgan started to force her expression into a semblance of the shock a Norm would feel, but when Harding raised an eyebrow, she dropped the act. Professional courtesy, in a way.

Harding continued, "I understand you found intel about possible IEDs at the Radcliffe residence? The younger Kroft brother, Paul, he's former military, used pipe bombs to gain access or as threats during several of their crimes. Liked to put a suicide vest on the children and make the adults go to the bank with his brother, withdraw their life savings. And then they'd kill them all anyway."

The brothers, young, physically fit, they would be a force to be reckoned with. Clint would need to walk a fine line, creating the illusion that brothers were the ones calling the shots. It wasn't a game Clint would have the patience to play for long, so he'd want to kill them as soon as he no longer needed them. But two brothers like the Krofts, used to maintaining constant control even as they divided and conquered, would not be easy marks. No sheep, these two.

Since Morgan had already taken most of Clint's money, she'd left him with no resources. If he couldn't kill the brothers, couldn't buy them off, he was helpless and vulnerable...unless Gibson Radcliffe provided both money and an escape route. All those bomb making materials... Gibson had to have a plan—or rather Clint did. But what? Maybe the bombs were for the brothers, some big score they were planning?

Harding's cell rang at the same time as the landline. And most of the other

phones in the office. She answered,
listened, then asked, "Where?" She
circled a location on the map and grabbed
it, telling Morgan, "Wait here."

The room exploded into action as
Harding barked questions and men and
women tried to get her answers. There
was an officer down. No, there wasn't, but
an officer was involved in a shooting. No,
it was a sighting of the fugitives.
Conflicting reports spread across the
cubicles like wild fire.

Morgan didn't hesitate. She took
advantage of the momentary chaos to
sidle through the maze and into the rear
hall where the restrooms, staircase, and
fire exit were located. As she walked, she
dialed. Because the place on the map
Harding had circled was Clint's bank,
Crossroads.

Exactly where she'd sent Jenna.

CHAPTER 12

JENNA LET OSHIRO lead the way to the building's front door. She felt exposed, out here in the open, but took comfort in the knowledge that Oshiro's partner was covering them from her sniper's perch. Up close, she could see that the brick building was older than she'd first thought, dating from close to the turn of the last century. Yet it was well maintained, including a very modern biometric keypad beside the front entrance.

"Definitely not a church," she said, nodding to the keypad.

Oshiro had his hand on his weapon but used one finger and a jerk of his chin to indicate the laser sensors at the door and windows.

He reached for the door handle— old-fashioned bronze molded into a lion's head—but before he could complete the motion, the door opened from inside. It was a movement timed to throw visitors off balance. Oshiro didn't fall for it. Instead, he stood at the entrance, scanning the inside, blocking Jenna's view with his bulk.

After a long moment when he didn't move, she stepped to his right, her own hand on her weapon, and looked past him. A twenty-something redhead dressed in a slinky gold cocktail dress stood smiling at them both, a tray with two bubbling glasses of champagne extended toward Oshiro.

"Welcome to Crossroads." With her free hand, she gestured to the interior. "Please. Come inside."

Marble columns stood on either side of the entrance. Beyond them more marble, reminding Jenna of the lobby of a luxury hotel. Leather couches and chairs ringed the space, girls in low cut dresses waltzing between the furniture and the men who occupied it.

Now she saw why Oshiro had frozen, still on alert but not committing himself to an entry. Several of the men wore the emblems of outlaw motorcycle gangs. Not just one gang, either. In the narrow field of vision between Oshiro and the waitress, Jenna spotted a Mongrel, two Reapers, and a cadre of Visigoths.

The leather-clad bikers were all sworn enemies, yet they lounged, relaxed, chatting and flirting with the girls, no weapons in sight. Interspersed among the bikers were men clad in business suits, laptops and tablets or phones at hand, conferring with the bikers.

What the hell was this place? she wondered again. Ignoring Oshiro's scowl, Jenna stepped past him, inside the building, crossing beneath the twin marble columns.

"We've been expecting you, Ms. Galloway." The waitress extended the tray and Jenna took a glass of champagne,

using her non-shooting hand. Had Morgan
called to warn the people at Crossroads
that she was coming? Or maybe Clint
had? Could he have somehow known?
Was this a trap? She took a gulp of the
champagne, shivering as the bubbles went
down too fast and crackled against the
back of her throat.

"You can check your weapons here,"
the girl said, leading Jenna to a coat-
check counter beside the entrance.
Discreet paneled lockers covered the wall
behind another scantily clad young
woman.

Oshiro followed Jenna, his steps
reluctant, waving aside the champagne.
Jenna could feel his tension as he scanned
the room, not liking what he saw. She
followed his glance, past the lounging
bikers. A large, old-fashioned bank vault,
its tremendous round door standing open,
took up the back half of the building.
Inside, she could see what appeared to be
safety deposit boxes, each with a keypad.

"Morgan said it was a bank," she
murmured to Oshiro. "Guess she was
being literal."

"Your weapons, please," the waitress repeated, sounding annoyed at their dawdling.

"Federal agent," Oshiro answered. "I need to speak to—"

"Me, I suspect," another woman interrupted, coming up from behind the waitress. Dark-skinned with exotic features, she was dressed in an elegant black silk pantsuit that somehow managed to appear more sexy than any of the skimpy cocktail waitresses' dresses. "I'm Samra. Happy to help in any way I can. But we do not permit weapons in the public lounge."

"Deputy US Marshal Timothy Oshiro, ma'am. I'm here—"

Samra raised a hand. "I'm sure you're here with the best of intentions, Deputy Oshiro. But, as I said, we do not allow weapons in our common space." She gestured to the outlaw bikers who had all turned to gawk at the commotion, murmuring to each other with scowls etched into their faces. "I'm sure you can understand why, given our clientele."

Oshiro met her fake, unyielding

smile with one of his own. "And I'm sure you understand why, given your clientele, I'll be keeping my weapons."

"What is this place?" Jenna asked, unable to restrain her curiosity any further. "A bar? Bank? Brothel?"

Samra made a chagrined frown at the last. "Come with me. You can keep your weapons while we speak in my private office."

She led them past the coat check area and a polished walnut counter that seemed to serve both as a bar and a teller's desk to a room with dark paneling and elegant antique furniture. A man stood outside, obviously a guard, but he did not carry any weapons that Jenna could see. Samra waved them to luxurious leather chairs, while she settled herself behind her desk and steepled her fingers in thought. Jenna took a seat, smoothing her fingers across the baby soft fine leather, while Oshiro stood behind her.

"I'm sure you can appreciate that your presence here is quite unsettling to my clients. This is neutral ground, no matter which side of the law you're on. As long as you abide by the rules, all are welcome." She nodded to Oshiro. "Even a US Marshal. But we have rules for a reason. Mainly the safety of my people. I apologize if it offends, but I must insist that you relinquish your weapons for the duration of your visit."

The steely set of Oshiro's jaws told Jenna how unlikely that was. But she was no longer law enforcement; she was free to do what she wanted. Who cared, if it got her the answers she needed? She might even use Oshiro's recalcitrance to her advantage.

"You're Switzerland," she blurted out, the pieces falling into place. "Totally neutral. Providing a service to all."

"An essential service," Samra agreed. "We not only pride ourselves on attending to our customers' financial needs, we protect their privacy. Secure and confidential. That is the Crossroads way."

"I'm after Clinton Caine," Oshiro finally spoke. "He's a client of yours."

"I can neither confirm nor deny that."

"You're not actually *in* Switzerland," he reminded her. "We have federal statutes that regulate banks. I'm sure your customers would not appreciate it if I got a warrant to examine all of your records and open every safe deposit box."

Samra merely smiled. "You can try. But it won't be easy. We are a private equity corporation, not bound by the FDIC regulations."

"How does it work?" Jenna asked. "Let's say I wanted to open an account. Could you or one of your people give me a tour, show me what that would entail?"

"Of course, Ms. Galloway." Again Jenna was a bit freaked that they knew her name—but she refused to rise to the bait and ask how; it would be seen as a sign of weakness. Oshiro edged a glance her way, obviously wondering if she'd led him into some kind of trap. But so far, he seemed content to follow her lead.

Samra continued, "Someone of your background would definitely fit our client profile." Okay...so Samra knew more than Jenna's name, she knew who Jenna really was—more than what was reported in the newspapers. The banker had access to top-notch researchers. Or Morgan had told her. "But again, no weapons allowed in the public areas. Or the vault."

"Your associate out front, she said you were expecting me. How?"

"Another client suggested that you might be arriving sometime in the next few days."

"Another client? Clinton Caine? Or maybe his daughter, Morgan Ames?"

Samra didn't take the bait, merely smiled. "We've built our business on referrals. If you choose to utilize our services, you'll be afforded the same discretion."

Jenna stood. Oshiro straightened but didn't stop her. "All right. Show me how it all works." She unholstered her SIG from her belt then also retrieved her backup from its ankle holster and set them both on Samra's desk.

Samra arched an eyebrow. "The knife as well, please."

How the hell? Jenna leaned forward to slide free the knife concealed in her belt at the small of her back.

As she handed it to Samra, she twisted and caught a glimpse of the woman's tablet and saw an image of a human skeleton. Ah...the marble columns at the entrance concealed some kind of X-ray scanning equipment. Smart. Especially given Samra's clientele.

Samra tapped her tablet and spoke into it. "Heidi, would you be so kind as to give Ms. Galloway a tour?"

Moments later, the pretty redhead in the gold dress was leading Jenna away from the office and toward the bank vault. She'd swapped out the serving tray for a small tablet identical to Samra's. "Would you be interested in learning more about our off-shore holdings? I see here that you currently prefer the Caymans. I believe we could provide you with a more advantageous return on investment. Or are you looking for a physical facility to store cash deposits and other valuables?"

The bikers and their accountants had cleared out—Oshiro cramping their style, no doubt. Leaving only Jenna, the trio of waitresses—tellers? Financial advisors? Call girls?—the two visible security guards, bartender, and the coat check girl.

"Cash," Jenna answered.

Heidi nodded, moving past the counter toward the vault. "As you can see we offer top-notch physical security. The vault itself was designed in 1932 by Louis Simon, one of the architects who built Fort Knox."

Jenna paused at the thick vault door, stroking her hand along its edge. "Old school."

"Yes. But it's not the most impenetrable security feature." Heidi swept into the vault and waved her arm like a game show hostess revealing a prize. "We have a state-of-the-art intruder detection system, and each deposit box has its own eight-digit encryption key, programmed solely by the owner. If you'd like, we can also add biometric security at an additional cost."

Jenna stared at the keypads. Morgan's notation on the map started with three digits—304, the box number, no doubt—followed by eight more digits.

She moved beside box 304 but kept her gaze focused on the box diagonally above it, hoping to divert Heidi's attention from her real target. Box 304 had a regular keypad, no biometrics. Good.

All she needed now was a few seconds without Heidi watching her. "Is there an empty one you could demonstrate with? I'd like to examine the interior construction."

"Of course." While Heidi consulted her tablet and moved to a box toward the front of the vault, Jenna typed in the code Morgan had given her.

The box's door opened with a click. Heidi spun around. "What are you—"

Before she could finish, a blast rocketed through the air.

CHAPTER 13

MORGAN ESCAPED DOWN the rear hall and locked herself in the empty men's room. She kept dialing Jenna until finally someone answered.

"Jenna, are you okay?"

"What the hell, Morgan! You should have warned me."

"Of what? What happened?"

"Your father's lock box was rigged to blow. Would have taken my hand off if I'd been standing on the other side of the door."

"So, you're okay? Everyone's okay?"

"Yeah. I'm fine. Your banker friend

isn't too happy, though. I think she's going to want her toaster back." Toaster? Jenna always babbled when her adrenaline spiked.

As soon as the cops heard that there'd been an explosion at the location Morgan had sent Jenna to—no matter that it was Jenna who triggered it and Clint who planted the device—they'd want to hang on to Morgan. Which meant processing her. Fingerprints, photos, who knew what else? No way was she letting Jenna's stupid mistake put her in the system or land her behind bars.

Even if sooner or later they'd learn how wrong they were, Morgan knew better than to wait around for the scales of justice to right themselves. Besides, she'd gotten what she came for, she now knew where not to look for Clint.

She had a feeling none of his usual patterns fit—smart thinking on his behalf, but she was a bit surprised, since Clint was nothing but a creature of habit. Gibson Radcliffe. He was the key.

Time to move. She hung up the phone and opened the door, assessing her options. There was a fire exit, its red sign tempting her from her left, at the end of the hall. Wired to alarm when opened, which she could circumvent, given enough time, but why not use it to her advantage instead?

Directly across from her was another metal door leading into the stairwell. She closed her eyes, imagining the building's layout. The law offices would be directly overhead, the empty renovated area beside it. Yes, that would do nicely.

Voices from the main area grew louder and more strident as men and women grabbed weapons and equipment. Morgan skittered across the hall to the stairwell door. Locked, but not for long, thanks to the picks concealed in her sunglasses.

She propped it open—it locked automatically from this side, which worked to her favor—and sprinted to the fire exit, shoving the door open, throwing her purse out into the snow piled up along the edges of the parking lot. Blonde-Barbie-secretary's props scattered across the pavement, creating a trail. Perfect.

The fire exit alarm blared. She raced to the stairwell, pushed through that door, shut it, and ducked down below the glass window at the top, just as footsteps pounded past.

Then she raced up the stairs to the second floor. Entry to the side of the building being renovated was protected by sheets of plywood and a heavy door secured by a padlock. She could open it—but no way could she close it again when she was through, which would give them an easy trail to follow, once they began to search in earnest. Instead, she turned to the glass door at the lawyer's office with its gaudy parody of the old Uncle Sam recruiting poster. *In an accident? We get money for You!*

Should use some of that money for better locks, she thought as she opened the door and slipped through. No alarm, either. The lights were off in the office, and no sounds came as she entered. Out to a late lunch? In court? Chasing ambulances? Given the stack of overdue bills scattered below the mail slot, maybe they weren't even open anymore. She didn't really care.

She locked the door behind her and moved into the inner office that shared a common wall with the construction area. On the way here, she'd noticed the dumpster in the alley was filled with insulation—which meant there was probably nothing but drywall between her and her escape route. If she chose her access point correctly.

The lawyer's decorating skills were no better than his advertising. The drywall hadn't even been painted, was bare except for its original coat of primer. The only furniture was a cheap desk and a wheeled AV cabinet with outdated equipment, including a VCR.

She rolled the cabinet aside, knelt down close to the floor, and drew one of her knives, a serrated Kershaw Leek, tough enough to cut through bone. A sheet of cheap drywall was no match for it. In less than two minutes, she had a small door cut out of the wall between two studs, just large enough for her to wiggle through.

Good timing, because as she was

pulling the AV cabinet back in place to cover it, she heard pounding on the office's front door and a man's voice radioing in that the office appeared secure. She huddled, kneeling on the plywood subfloor, her head still inside the hole in the wall, studs on either side, one hand grasping the base of the AV cabinet, the other her knife.

Everything went silent. She finished creeping backwards into the half-demolished space. The exterior walls were intact, but everything else had been stripped, leaving exposed studs, dangling wires, floorboards littered with debris. One window was removed, the opening filled with a yellow plastic chute. She eyed it. It wasn't a gentle slope down to the dumpster, rather a straight drop. She might be better off climbing down the outside of the building.

She glanced out the other windows, taking care to stay hidden. Cop cars with light bars rolling red and white waited at the main entrance and the rear parking lot. If she tried to climb down the alley wall, she'd be totally exposed. How long would they search for her?

She needed a vehicle but had to get clear of the cops before she stole one. Sliding her phone free, she considered. Not Andre—first, he'd be surrounded by cops at Gibson's house, and second, he'd be on Jenna's side, want Morgan to do the right thing, trust the cops to figure things out. As if that ever actually worked.

Micah. He didn't live far from here, and no one would ever suspect him. All she needed was twenty minutes of his time, and she'd be gone.

Still...she actually had doubts. A twinge of remorse. So unlike her. It wasn't that she didn't trust that Micah would come through, it was that she knew he would. And she hated getting him involved in anything to do with Clint, no matter how remote.

Clint could never know about Micah. But it wasn't like Clint was anywhere near here. Micah would be safe. She hit the speed dial. "Hey. Got a few minutes? I could use your help—and a ride."

"Sure," he said. So trusting. She worried that someday it might get him killed—it'd already gotten his neck sliced open and him thrown in juvie for something he didn't do. Maybe it was good she was in his life, if only to watch out for him.

She gave Micah directions and removed her pink coat. As much as she liked it—despite it being absolutely not Morgan's style, it was the first time she'd ever been complimented on something she'd worn—it was way too visible. Even if she turned it inside out, the lining was a shiny silver that would do her no favors. She shivered. Carried the coat over to the window with the debris chute.

The plastic tunnel rippled in the wind but seemed fairly sturdy—it would need to be to handle construction trash. She poked her head inside, assessing the drop and what lay at the bottom, but it was too dark to see. She could be jumping into a dumpster filled with broken glass and twisted metal beneath the fiberglass insulation, who knew?

Maybe the coat could come in handy after all. She wadded it into a ball and stuffed it down the chute. Then she climbed in, feet first, face to the room, and hung by her hands from the bottom of the window frame. The plastic chute was slippery, no way to get a handhold. Nothing to do but take a leap of faith.

She let go and fell.

CHAPTER 14

GIBSON ALMOST DIDN'T need the car's heater. The glow of triumph after following the cops and Morgan here to their squalid little manhunt HQ and now sitting right across the parking lot watching them get nowhere was more than enough to keep him warm. Clint wanted the girl, but instead of playing the game, following the trail of clues he'd left her, Morgan had brought the cops into his mother's house—into Gibson's home—and now he was having fun imagining other fates for Morgan Ames.

The other convicts, the two brothers

waiting impatiently for Clint to bring them their payment for busting him out, the ones who jeered at Gibson every time he went to replenish their supply of beer and pizza, they'd reward him handsomely if he took Morgan to them. They wouldn't be foolish enough to kill her—not if they wanted their money from Clint—but they'd teach her a lesson, that's for sure. Pretty young thing like Morgan...oh, what they'd do to her.

No way in hell would Clint want her as his partner after that.

Two birds. Instead of taking Morgan directly to Clint, he'd deliver her to the brothers. He held their trust, barely, but that was waning with every day that Clint hadn't delivered the money he'd promised them. Morgan would keep them happy and occupied until Gibson could prove to Clint that he was the worthy one, not her. All he needed was another day, just one more day. Then Clint—hell, the whole damned world—would know once and for all that he was his father's son, capable of the same awful greatness as Clinton Caine.

Imagining Clint's expression of awe and pride when he saw how Gibson had taken Clint's simple plan and made it so much greater added to Gibson's satisfaction. He would show them, show them all exactly who Gibson Radcliffe really was. And all he needed was to get his hands on Clint's precious baby girl.

The back door of the building flew open, startling him from his fantasies. Morgan appeared briefly, tossing a purse out into the snow, then vanished again. Gibson hunched down, out of sight, angling the mirrors to watch. A minute or so later, cops came clumping through the doors—both the front and the rear, circling around, obviously looking for someone.

Morgan. What the hell was she up to? He shifted the car into gear and pulled out, turning into the alley beside the building, inching past the construction dumpster then turning onto the main road, most of his attention still watching the building in his rearview mirror.

The cops set up patrol cars at the front and rear doors. Several officers scoured the parking lot, checking each car, while others drove away, lights flashing but no sirens.

Gibson circled the block. By the time he returned to his starting point, the cops had cleared the parking lot, leaving only a pair at each exit. Morgan was still inside the building. How long would it take for them to find her? Where would she go? Would she hide like a coward or did she have a plan?

He drove around the block one more time, making sure no one was paying attention to him, then parked, this time in front of a nail salon in the strip mall across the street. He couldn't see the doors to the building as well as he had from his first vantage point, but Morgan wouldn't be coming through them, he was sure. Instead, he focused on the side alley.

After a few minutes with no activity at the building, he wondered if he'd lost her when he'd been circling the block. But then a red car slowed and turned into the alley, parking beside the dumpster.

A cascade of pink insulation rose up,

and Morgan appeared, her pink coat draped over her head and shoulders, making her almost impossible to see until she shook her dark hair loose. A guy jumped out of the car, climbed up onto its trunk, and helped lift Morgan out of the dumpster.

It was all over in a few seconds. But not so fast that Gibson didn't catch the way the driver hugged Morgan, despite the fiberglass covering her, or the possessive hand planted against the small of her back as he escorted her into his car.

They pulled out of the alley, Gibson following them. Morgan was Clint's weak spot, and he knew how to put her to good use. Especially now that he'd found Morgan's weak spot: Mr. Driver, her Sir Galahad, riding to her rescue.

He slapped the steering wheel and cranked up the Slayer playing on the stereo. This was going to be so much fun!

CHAPTER 15

"WHERE TO?" MICAH asked as he steered his Ford Focus onto route 22 and drove away from the improvised police command post. Morgan was slouched down low below the dash, covered by her coat, strands of pink fiberglass itching. The coat had saved her from too much exposure to the noxious fibers and had protected her from the bits of drywall below the insulation. She might have a few bruises from her leap of faith but nothing worse. Except she'd lost one of her knives, her favorite CQC blade, during the fall.

Once they were past the two traffic lights with cameras, she climbed up onto the front seat and answered Micah's question. "Anywhere there's a parking lot."

They weren't that far from the mall—always a good place to go car shopping. Although this time of day, that usually meant the employee vehicles parked in the rear, far from any security. Morgan hated taking cars from worker bees just trying to earn. Not only did the owners miss them immediately, they were usually crap cars. Which was why she normally picked up cars from the airport long-term parking—also convenient for returns, not to mention free housing for the duration. Once she had the owners' name and address, learning details of their itinerary was child's play.

"There." She pointed to the entrance to a warehouse store sitting in the middle of a shopping center. Not the best place to grab a new set of wheels, but there was an office building beside it with a small parking garage. After she left Micah, that's where she'd head.

He made the turn, pulled into an empty parking space at the far edge of the lot where a few scraggly bushes posing as landscaping gave them some semblance of privacy.

"All that stuff back there," Micah started. "Who were you running from? Why were the cops there?"

No sense hiding a truth he could learn for himself with thirty seconds and Google. "Those were the cops looking for Clinton Caine and the other escaped prisoners."

"Clinton Caine? The serial killer?" He undid his seatbelt so that he could turn to face her.

Morgan thought about running—it was her default and usually served her well—but something held her back. She wished she knew exactly what it was and why she couldn't ignore it.

"What's Caine have to do with you? You didn't cross his path during one of your cases, did you?" As far as Micah knew, Morgan was an emancipated minor working with investigators who put her especially youthful looks to good use by sending her undercover. Close to the truth but also so very, very far away.

She hesitated. Debated not answering. How far could she trust him?

"Morgan. Tell me the truth. I want to know. Everything." His ice-blue eyes bore into her. He wasn't asking a question, yet he was asking the most important question of all.

Morgan considered her response carefully. She knew what she wanted to say, knew exactly the words to use to convince him his suspicions were wrong. She had one hand on the car door, ready to bolt.

But then she turned to face him, pulling her knees up to her chest, so close that his face filled her vision—yet also very far apart, separated by far more than a gear shift. She wanted to trust him. Needed to trust him. With the truth.

Even if it meant losing him.

"Clinton Caine is my father." The words hung between them, long enough that she imagined them sprouting devil's horns and wings as they jeered at her. "He raised me. I've never been to school—

not since third grade. Never been around kids or a mother or, really, not anyone at all. Except Clint."

Micah was smart—especially about people. So it was no surprise he understood everything behind her words. His breath escaped him with a whooshing sound and he pulled both fists into his belly as if he'd been sucker punched. Despite the weatherman's optimistic predictions, it was cold enough outside that their breathing quickly fogged the windows, creating a cocoon of intimacy.

"Clint didn't want a daughter," she continued, without mercy for herself or him. Funny, she didn't feel hot or cold, not even scared. Just weary. Relieved she wouldn't have to carry on this charade of pretending to be a normal human girl with normal human emotions.

"He wanted a partner," Micah finished for her. "I read about him. About what he did."

She nodded. Waited for him to run— it's what she would do if their situations were reversed.

Micah didn't run. He reached across

the space that separated them, tugged at her hand, and pressed it to his heart. He felt so warm—or maybe it was simply that she was so numb.

"Those women he kidnapped and tortured. He made you part of that?"

"Yes." The word sounded so tiny and harmless. But with it she surrendered everything. "He taught me how to fish—that was his word for it. Going fishing. Using me as bait. When I got good at that, he taught me how to do...other things to his precious little fish. He liked the way I could make them scream."

She felt his body stiffen beneath her palm, absorbing the blow. "Did *you* like it?"

How to explain? "I liked being good at something. When Clint was happy with me, with what I did, it was as if God had reached down and handed me the whole universe wrapped in a ribbon. I lived to make him smile."

"He conditioned you. Taught you."

"Yes. But I think I'm also wired like he is. I'm not like normal people. Somehow I'm different inside. I don't feel things the same way you do. I'm...empty."

She blinked. That was something she'd never admitted before, not even to herself. She'd always told herself that being different meant being special, that not feeling made her superior to the sheep and fish that filled this world. But after meeting Micah, all that changed. Not who she was—that was hardwired. Rather, who she *wanted* to be.

It wasn't merely that Morgan trusted Micah—she also trusted Andre but still never let her guard totally drop when she was around him. No. This was much, much worse than that.

Micah made her feel safe.

Except now he was shaking his head. It was too much for him. He'd be leaving her soon, she was certain.

"Did you," he swallowed and started again. "Did you kill anyone?"

"Yes." Her tone was as blunt as a two-by-four. "And I enjoyed it—it's the one thing I'm good at."

A frown pulled his eyebrows together and he turned to face her again, a hand on each of her elbows, gripping her tight. "No. Morgan, that's not true. I understand—kinda—what you're telling me. I can only imagine what it was like, growing up that way. But you can't truly believe that. You're so smart and brave and—look what you did when we first met. You saved my life. Not just mine. And you did it without killing anyone."

Before she could protest, he pulled her in close and kissed her. It wasn't as sweet as their first kiss, or as tentative. This time it was Micah telling her what he felt, what he believed but did not have the words for.

Morgan couldn't help herself. She wrapped her arms around him, wanting more.

Finally they parted. She traced a finger along the scar on his neck, brushed his hair away from his face. "You should leave. Me. Now. Forever."

"No." He lay his hand over hers, pressing her palm against his cheek.

"Seriously. Micah. I'm selfish and impulsive, and I'll always put my needs before anyone else's, and I'm manipulative, and—"

"And brilliant and courageous and the strongest damn person I've ever met. Besides, you should know a few things about me."

His eyes were like twinkling stars, and she couldn't resist. "Oh, yeah? What's hiding in that deep, dark past of yours, Micah Chase?"

"I'm a slob. I don't put the toilet seat down. I like to argue and can see three sides to every debate, and I'll take them all at the same time. I live inside my head and lose track of time and am always late. And I'm selfish." He kissed her forehead tenderly. "Extremely selfish. And stubborn. Once I find something worth hanging on to, I'll never ever let go."

He pulled her against his chest, his lips brushing the top of her head as she listened to his heartbeat. Faster than hers but steady and strong.

"We're a pair, aren't we?" she whispered.

Before he could answer, the door behind Morgan opened and a man hopped in, brandishing a pistol. "Don't move, or Prince Charming here is dead."

CHAPTER 16

THE EXPLOSION IN Clint's vault hadn't injured Jenna, but it had frightened her. More than she cared to admit. Oshiro had decided it wasn't even a blasting cap, rather just a few M-80 firecrackers tied to a clever sparking tool with short fuses. Given the narrow confines of the bank box, the force of the explosion had been contained, creating far more sound than fury or damage.

Tell that to her pounding heart or the fuzzy way her hearing kept getting way too loud and then would cut out, the world silenced by white noise. Or the trembles that didn't shake her body but instead radiated below her skin like an itch that couldn't be scratched but made her flesh crawl.

At least after experiencing Clint's treachery firsthand, Samra had been willing to sacrifice client confidentiality. She'd given them access to all of Clint's accounts—which now added up to less than a thousand dollars in total, not including whatever cash he'd stashed in his deposit box.

From the records, it seemed someone had drained the online accounts while Clint was in custody. Jenna had a damn good idea who that was but said nothing to Oshiro. He was more interested in Clint's last visit to the bank in person—two days ago. Their security records had footage of Clint coming and going—there were no cameras inside the vault, although after Clint's stunt, Jenna guessed that would soon change—as well as video of his vehicle, a silver Camry.

Most interesting, he hadn't been alone. Two people had accompanied him. One was a fellow escapee, Paul Kroft, the younger of the two convict brothers who'd escaped with Clint. And a teenaged kid. Jenna didn't recognize him, but after talking with Andre and learning what he and Jenna had found at the Radcliffe residence, she texted him a photo. He confirmed her hunch.

Gibson Radcliffe. Playing chauffeur to two escaped killers.

"Whatever Clint's planning, it can't be anything good," she told Oshiro after she collected her weapons and they returned to the Tahoe. This time she let Oshiro drive, pretended it was because she needed to stay on her phone to follow up with Andre, but she was pretty sure he saw through her deception.

While they drove, she updated Oshiro on Gibson Radcliffe and the evidence of his involvement with Clint's escape.

"So Clint grooms Gibson, coerces him to help facilitate the escape?" Oshiro said.

"From what Andre says about the kid's journal entries, doesn't sound like it took a whole lot of convincing."

"Clint uses the funds he has access to and covers the supplies, transpo, probably a place for them to lay low..."

"Them? You think he's still with the others?"

"Why else would one of the brothers accompany Clint to the bank? My guess is the brothers were the muscle behind the escape, and they didn't do it out of the goodness of their hearts. They were expecting to be paid. Also explains why Clint chose them to partner with. Paul has experience with IEDs, and Pete worked in the prison's infirmary."

"Where he stole the drugs they used on the guards." Clint and the others had escaped while en route to the courthouse. Always the weakest link in any incarceration: prisoner transport to outside facilities.

"Yes. We're still looking into the attorneys involved—but my bet's on someone in the courthouse. Whoever scheduled all of their court appearances for the same day. Not my team's brief, so I don't have details. But Clint has absolutely no history of using explosives—

certainly nothing along the lines of the plans your partner found at Gibson's." Oshiro tapped the steering wheel in thought.

"I'll bet it was the younger brother, Paul, who taught him how to rig that little surprise package back in the bank."

"A few firecrackers is nothing compared to what they could build with the supplies Gibson ordered. Which takes us to a whole other level. We're not just talking bombs to be used to defend their hidey-hole or as a diversion."

"I think you might need to get the ATF guys taking a real close look at what a guy with Paul Kroft's background could build with the stuff Gibson obtained."

"On it." He steered with one hand as he grabbed his phone. A few minutes later he hung up after a conversation that was extremely one-sided with Oshiro doing the listening. "It's not good. We're talking some major damage and multiple devices."

"What kind of damage? As much as the Boston Marathon?"

"More like Oklahoma City. If they

use all of their supplies." He blew his breath out. "I don't get it. None of these guys have any indications of terroristic inclinations. They aren't radicals. The Kroft brothers are hyper-violent meth heads always looking and failing to find a big score. And your guy, Caine, he's a psycho-sexual sadist. What the hell are they doing playing with bombs? They should be out there running for the nearest sunny beach in a country without extradition. Or holing up in a nice, quiet farmhouse, waiting for things to die down."

"Seems like they don't want things to die down. They want to make some noise. A lot of it."

"But why? And when and where?"

"Not to mention: how many people are going to die?" she finished for him.

"None. Not on my watch."

"There's only one place to start. The kid."

He jerked his chin in agreement. "We need to put this Gibson kid and everything he's touched under a microscope." He dialed his phone once more. "I want to know where and who this kid's been in contract with for every second of every day since he first reached out to Caine," he ordered.

Oshiro listened, tensed, then said, "On our way."

"What?"

"Someone just phoned in a bomb threat to the kid's school."

She glanced at the clock on the dash. "It's real."

"What makes you so certain?"

"No one calls in a fake threat at two-thirty on a Friday. School's just getting ready to let out for the weekend. Defeats the purpose."

He gave a small grunt that told her he'd already figured that out for himself. "That's what worries me. We have no clue what's really behind anything these guys are doing."

CHAPTER 17

MORGAN WHIRLED TO face the threat but then stopped. She knew the man—boy, really. Gibson Radcliffe. How the hell? She slid her hand toward her knife. Gibson aimed the gun at Micah, but his dead-eyed stare and goofy grin were solely for Morgan.

"Think I don't know what you're thinking, sis?" He arched an eyebrow in disapproval. "Hands on the dash."

Micah tensed, preparing to make a move. Morgan shook her head no, keeping his gaze as she raised her hands and planted them on the dash. Resentment flashed through Micah's eyes, but he nodded and followed her lead. Probably because he remembered how she'd saved them before when they first met and were in trouble. Mostly because he trusted her. Trusting. Micah's weakness. She hoped this time it wouldn't get him killed.

"What do you want?" Micah asked. His voice didn't sound like him, carried a touch of the wolf.

Gibson's smile grew wider and weirder if that was possible. "Car parked at the edge of the lot, windows all steamed—did I interrupt something?"

This usually would have been when Morgan slit someone's throat, but that was off the table, not when she had to protect Micah. She wasn't used to that, having someone to protect. Cramped her style. Except that Micah wouldn't even be here if it wasn't for her. That thought brought with it an uncertain and unfamiliar twinge of something deep in her gut...guilt? Was this what guilt felt like?

Her self-analysis was cut short when Gibson fished a loop of cable wire from his pocket and handed it to Micah. "Put this around your neck."

Before Morgan could stop him, Micah obeyed. The wire was a quarter inch thick, run through a loop to create a noose. Gibson yanked the cable tight—it made a zipping noise as it hummed through the loop—and pulled Micah back into his seat until his body was arched up and he was struggling to loosen the cable, now a garrote, from around his throat.

"Stop," Morgan ordered. "I know who you are, and I know what you want." Gibson stared at her, yanking the cable tighter, Micah made a small strangling noise as his face turned red and he fought to breathe. "Let him go, and I'll give you what you want."

Gibson pursed his lips in exaggerated thought then released the garrote enough for Micah to breathe. "He's handy to have around. I think I'll keep him. Make sure you behave yourself. Does he have a name?"

Every fiber of Morgan's being wanted to slice that twisted grin from Gibson's face then carve out a new smile for him, one that wrapped all the way around his neck. But she restrained herself—if she couldn't control herself, no way would she be able to control the situation. She pulled in a breath. "Micah. His name is Micah."

"Micah." Gibson ran his fingers through Micah's hair and patted his head as if he were a dog. Despite the garrote, Micah tensed, his hands tightening into fists. Morgan risked Gibson's wrath, lowering one of her hands over Micah's, trying to reassure him.

"We're going to have some fun today." Gibson's voice turned sing-song as if he'd been rehearsing for this moment all his life. Maybe he actually was one of Clint's sons, because he sounded eerily like Clint right now.

"First, a pretty necklace for the lady." He handed Morgan her own wire noose. "Go on, put it on."

As he spoke, he wrenched Micah's tighter. Morgan complied. Gibson took the long ends of the cables in one hand, like reins, effectively controlling them in tandem. But in doing so, he released

Micah, so Morgan was happy with that small gain.

"Now some nice bracelets." He rummaged in a small backpack and brought out a handful of zip ties. "Morgan, wrists together, behind you. Micah, will you do the honors?"

She leaned forward and held her wrists up. Micah slid the plastic fastener over them and pulled gently, taking his time, his fingers caressing hers as if trying to impart some secret message.

"Tighter," Gibson ordered.

Micah inched the ties the slightest bit tighter. He couldn't know it, but it would actually be easier for Morgan to break free of them if they had no slack. As it was, they were just tight enough to restrain her and not tight enough for her to easily escape. She'd need to find a way to reach one of her barrettes—their steel fasteners could be used as shims on handcuffs or zip ties. But she couldn't act until she had a few minutes away from Gibson's scrutiny.

"Now, Micah, your turn. Tie your left wrist to the steering wheel, please."

Morgan slumped back in her seat and watched as Micah obeyed, his movements jerky, uncertain. Despite three people breathing inside it, the car was growing clammy with chill, and her coat had slid off her lap when she moved to allow Micah to restrain her.

"Where's Clint?" she asked, hoping to distract Gibson, keep his focus on her, not Micah.

"You think I'm going to deliver you straight to him? Is that what you want?" He searched her expression. "No. It's not what you want, is it? But it's what Clint wants." He seemed puzzled by her reluctance to rejoin Clint. "Tell you what. I think we're going to have some fun first. Show Clint what his little girl has become. Weak and pathetic. Not worthy."

"But you are?" she guessed.

"More than you," he snapped. He turned to search through his backpack, appearing to absentmindedly heave his weight against both garrotes, tightening them. Except there was nothing absentminded about it.

"Now...where is it?" He hummed a

little tune, his hand jerking the wire cables in time with the music, Morgan and Micah were reduced to mere marionettes fighting for their next breath. Then he emerged with a small glass vial filled with cloudy colorless liquid. "Ah...here we go."

He relaxed the wire cables. Morgan twisted her body to face Micah. She hated that he was here, going through this because of her. She needed him to know that she'd find a way out of this...but not right away. Not if that vial contained what she thought it did.

As she tried to force all of her feelings into an expression he could understand, Micah surprised her by giving her the most beautiful smile she'd ever seen. His lips barely moved at all, but his eyes—those gorgeous eyes that had first enchanted her—his eyes said it all. Vowed to fight, vowed to save her, vowed to die, if need be.

"No," she uttered the word despite herself. "Micah, do as he says. Exactly as he says. Everything will be all right."

Gibson popped his head between the two back seats, rolling his eyes first at

Micah, then at Morgan, then back to Micah. "You two love birds up to something?"

"Micah has nothing to do with this." One last attempt, futile as she knew it would be. Gibson may or may not have been Clint's biological son, but he definitely had Clint's nose for finding weakness in his victims. "Let him go, and I'll do anything you want."

"But if I keep him, you'll do it anyway. Besides, I have a friend waiting, and he's so very lonely. Been locked up without companionship for a long, long time. Might run into his brother as well, we'll see."

The other escaped convicts. She'd assumed Clint had either killed them or sent them on their own paths, fodder for the cops. If they were alive, and Clint wasn't with them...there must be some leverage in there somewhere. All she needed was to find a bargaining chip to save Micah's life.

Gibson dangled the vial between her and Micah.

"Clint gave me the recipe." The

strange smirk still danced across his lips. "You remember how it goes, right, Morgan? Playing with the fish he caught. So scared...those first sweet, sweet screams. He'd tell them he'd kill whoever they loved most, hunt them down and slice and dice them as the poor little fishy watched."

His eyes narrowed. "I'll bet you helped with that part, am I right? He told me how much you love your blades. Did he do the talking and watching while you filleted those fish, Morgan? Just a tiny slice here and there. Make them believe. Make them want to drink. I'm not as good with the knives as you are." His gaze edged back toward Micah. "But maybe all I need is practice."

"No." The word came out much higher pitched than she wanted.

Gibson's head jerked toward her as if he was a fish she'd hooked. Control, she needed to stay in control. She took a deep breath, swallowed her fear—it still strangled, caught in her throat, a fist trying to punch its way out. That was all right, because if she was going to save

Micah, she needed a bit of fear. To help her play the fish Gibson thought he'd snared...even as she reeled him in.

"No," she repeated, this time letting fear leach into her voice. It wasn't her own life she was afraid for. Which actually only made her more frightened. The fact that she'd let someone get close enough to her that she actually felt such a powerful need to protect them. Micah. He was the center of her fear, right now the center of her entire universe. "I'll drink it. Just don't hurt him."

"Good fishy." He held the vial above her lips, forcing her to tilt her head back and open her mouth beneath it as he released the sedative. "Night-night, tiny fish. Hope and pray I keep my promise and don't kill you both while you sleep."

She choked down the bitter tonic. Now came the hard part, the absolute most terrifying role she'd ever played: helpless, powerless, at his mercy until she woke again.

If she woke again.

When she woke again, she corrected firmly, the drug already muddling her thoughts. Except for one last, crystal clear revelation. To her surprise it wasn't a promise of revenge or image of how she would kill Gibson and enjoy watching him die.

No. Her final thought before blackness took her was hope.

Surprising because it was an emotion foreign to her. Morgan never wasted time or energy on empty wishes or dreams. She lived in the real world and made do with what was right there in front of her. She knew what she wanted and she got it—one way or the other. No wishful thinking involved.

But now, for the first time in her life, she clung to hope, sorry, weak thread of a lifeline that it was. Hope that Micah understood. Hope that he could stay strong until she woke and they were together again.

Hope that she could live long enough to save him.

CHAPTER 18

ONCE GIBSON HAD the girl subdued, the boy toy, Micah, was no problem, not at all. A bit of a letdown, in fact, how easy it was to control him with just a twitch on the noose around Morgan's unconscious throat. They drove out past the mall, first passing some light industrial parks, then a few downtrodden mobile home communities, finally turning off the main road and heading up into forests peppered with a few scattered small farms, each more isolate than the last and most all of them abandoned, awaiting either foreclosure or demolition.

He directed Micah up the gravel drive to the house he'd found for Clint and the two brothers. It was his mom's uncle's before they had to put him in a nursing home two years ago, but he refused to sign it over for the family to sell, so it sat empty. As if it'd just been waiting for Gibson to put it to good use.

The car hadn't even stopped before the door from the house banged open and the older brother rushed out, shotgun at the ready.

"Just me, just me," Gibson called as he opened his door, one hand still gripping the two cables that tethered his prisoners. "Brought you some appetizers before tonight's main event. Are Clint and your brother here?"

"No. They called, said you're to meet them at the staging area. Said you should take the Toyota, they're in the SUV." The brother pushed past Gibson and yanked open the driver's door, aiming his shotgun at the guy and then Morgan. "She dead? Clint's not gonna like that." He whirled on Gibson, the shotgun following the motion. "You better not have ruined this deal for us. If she's dead, Clint won't pay—"

"She's not dead. Just a little chemical restraint."

"What the hell you thinking, bringing her here? Clint said—"

"Think about it. If you have her, it guarantees you the money." Gibson restrained an eye roll as he argued with the older brother. Pete. No, Paul. No, Pete. Either way they were both idiots.

The way they refused to let Clint out of their sight, hounding him for their money, always one brother with him. Wasting Clint's time when he should be helping Gibson. After all, everything Gibson was doing, he was doing for Clint. No matter. After tonight it would all be over and both brothers dead. But in the meantime... "She's the key to Clint, and the boy's the key to her. Break one and you break them all."

Pete considered that, grabbed his phone, and called his brother, filling him in. His other hand—the one with the shotgun—didn't waver. "At least having her and the kid will relieve the boredom, if nothing else."

Gibson didn't need the help of a speaker to hear Paul's answer. "So would a stick in the eye, don't make me poke you with one."

"I'm just saying, if Clint's got in his head to double-cross us, no way in hell will he leave his girl behind. She's all I ever heard him talk about. Getting back to her, having fun like they used to." He made it sound like it was his idea to capture Morgan. Gibson bristled but held his silence. Clint still needed the brothers, which meant so did Gibson.

"Well, don't have too much fun. She's no good to us dead."

"I say it's more than time we get to have some fun. I'm so damned tired of sitting around here looking at your ugly ass."

"At least it's not as ugly as your fat face."

"Just let Clint know we're done playing around. He gets us our money. Tonight. Or his precious little girl is ours for the keeping."

"You get the job done downtown?" Paul meant the arena where the Pitt game was being held tonight.

"Yeah, they're all good to go. Still think I should come with the kid, back you up." He eyed Gibson with suspicion. "In case Clint tries to double-cross us."

"No. Now that we have the girl, that's not going to happen. Wait there with her. Gotta go, he's coming." Paul hung up.

Pete pocketed the phone then swiveled his head to regard Gibson. "And what am I going to do with you? Can't have you roaming around, playing peeping Tom while I introduce myself to our guests."

Gibson didn't like the glint in Pete's eye—sometimes the brothers forgot that it was Gibson responsible for them being free as well as Clint. He wished Clint had just killed them back at the truck stop where he'd picked them up after they killed the guards. But Clint said he needed at least one of them alive to play fall guy, clear his and Gibson's escape after tonight.

"Don't worry about me, I'm headed out. Gotta stay on schedule. Big night tonight."

"Better be. You know the reward on Clint's up to six figures. Me and Paulie, we'd best clear at least that with this score of yours. Otherwise..." He didn't finish his threat. Didn't have to.

Gibson turned and headed toward the carport where the silver Toyota waited. He made sure he was out of Pete's sight before he let his feelings show through. He wanted to be confident like Clint, unafraid of the risks he was taking, certain of the outcome. But so much could go wrong, and the stakes were so high.

At least he wouldn't have to worry about Pete coming after him. Between the two hostages, he was sure Pete would be well occupied until the job was done and he and Clint were long gone.

Poor Morgan. She was in for a rough night of it. Pete might have orders not to kill her, but no one ever said anything about not killing her Sir Galahad—or making her watch.

CHAPTER 19

JENNA AND OSHIRO arrived at the school and parked outside the police cordon. Most of the kids were gone, except for a bunch who mingled with other civilians beyond the barricades. The Allegheny County bomb squad was there along with the county's mobile command center, taking point, but Jenna also saw a Pittsburgh city K9 unit and one of their own bomb squad's tactical vans as well as patrol cars from the Monroeville PD.

Oshiro strode through the crowd of law enforcement like Moses parting the Red Sea, Jenna bobbing along in his wake.

The hopeful warm spring air was rapidly being replaced by gusting winds that carried the promise of rain and snow. Despite the cornucopia of cop cars from various jurisdictions, Oshiro led her unerringly to the two things any cop needed: intel and a hot cup of coffee.

They found both inside the mobile command center where Andre and a state trooper were briefing the locals on what they knew about Gibson. When the statie finished, Oshiro introduced her to Jenna as Corporal Harding—"Call me Liz," she interrupted him—and handed Jenna off to her while he joined Andre at the bank of monitors focused on the search inside the school.

Jenna quickly filled Liz in on what little she knew—well, what little she was willing to share—and watched as Oshiro and Andre quickly bonded over their joysticks and gadgets, conducting an entire conversation via monosyllabic utterances and the occasional chin jerk.

"Guys," Liz said. "Always with the tribal bonding and alpha dog sniffing." She shrugged and sipped her coffee.

"Whatever gets the job done."

The RV was small enough that there was no way Oshiro and Andre couldn't hear her, but the only indication that they did was Oshiro shrugging one shoulder. Liz seemed to translate that as "Come here, we've found something," and the two women moved closer until they could watch the screens over the men's shoulders.

To Jenna's surprise, they weren't monitoring the progress of the bomb techs but rather video feeds of security cameras dating back the past week.

"Principal said there'd been no alarms and no record of Gibson being on the premises at all this week. We had their security company give us access so we could see for ourselves," Liz explained.

"What about the bomb?" Jenna asked.

"Oh, it's there. Hiding in plain sight." Andre switched something on the monitor to reveal a live feed of a long hallway that ended in a set of double doors. A robot was making its way slowly down the hall; the camera he'd accessed must have been a body cam on a bomb tech's suit.

"Where?"

"Inside the fire extinguisher. Kid emptied out the real one, replaced it. Big question is what with," Oshiro said.

"And what the trigger device is," Andre finished for him. "Gibson's shopping list included European camp stove tablets."

Damn. The tablets were made of hexamine—a popular detonating agent among amateur bomb makers and terrorists.

"They'll handle the bomb," Liz told Jenna. "Our concern is when it was placed. If it was sometime in the past day, we can track the kid's movements, maybe get a lead on where he was going."

"Which means a lead on where Clint is."

"Exactly. If your theory is correct and the kid is our convicts' conduit to the outside world, then he's the key to finding them."

"Except we're not seeing anything on the security footage," Andre said.

"Not for today, at least," Oshiro confirmed, still scrolling through the sped-up footage of the hallway.

"Go back through the entire week," Liz ordered, but Jenna heard the sigh in her voice. Going into their fourth day of the manhunt—which no doubt meant four days without sleep, proper food, or any hopeful answers, it had to be exhausting.

"In the meantime, we should come at this from another direction. Any word on the girl?" Liz called the question to one of the other cops in the front of the RV.

"Morgan?" Jenna asked. "She's not in custody?"

"Didn't have a chance to tell you," Andre answered, the blur of security footage grainy as it sped past his monitor. "She ran."

"After we got word of the explosion you were involved in," Liz added.

"I'd hardly call it an explosion. A few firecrackers, that's all." Last thing Jenna needed was the fugitive task force to think she was stupid or careless enough to set off an IED.

"Still," Liz said, "after Oshiro and Lester called it in, the girl left. No one's seen her since. We're not even sure exactly how she got past us."

"Get used to it," Jenna said, glad she wasn't the only one who found Morgan's propensity to vanish in plain sight irritating. "Morgan does what Morgan wants. She probably got bored and ran off to meet up with her new boyfriend."

Morgan thought she was being so sly and secretive about Micah—except for the part where she'd asked Andre for advice, and of course, Andre had then told Jenna. Silly man, he'd thought it a sign that Morgan could change, that she had a trace of human feelings.

Andre glanced up at that. "Not a bad idea. We should call Micah. He might know something."

"You call him." Jenna had met the kid after Morgan had saved his life and had been barely able to coax two words from him. "He'll talk to you."

Andre looked to Liz, who nodded her approval. Leaving the video console in Oshiro's hands, he stepped to the front of the RV where it was quieter and sat down in the driver's seat with his phone. He was only gone a few moments when all of the law enforcement comms filled with the tense voices of excited cops. Footsteps pounded past the RV, and men shouted in the distance. Liz turned the monitor feed back to the live action.

The robot had reached the bomb and X-rayed it with its portable unit. The X-ray filled the screen with wires and circuitry that Jenna couldn't interpret. But there was no mistaking the dismay that filled Oshiro's face—the fact that he was showing any emotion told her just how bad it was.

Only the bomb tech stayed calm, his voice slow and steady. He seemed a bit impressed by the challenge before him. "Folks, hope you're seeing this," he said, not quite whistling in appreciation. "Because this baby is a beauty."

When she'd worked with the Postal Service, Jenna had dealt with enough cases of mail bombs to know that when a bomb tech was in awe of a bomb maker's creation it was most definitely not a good thing.

She had the sudden urge to volunteer her and Andre's services to go on a food run. Anything to get far, far away from the evil contraption whose innards were displayed on the screen.

"Is that what I think it is?" she asked, nodding to the chemical composition supplied by the electronic sniffer.

"HMTD," Oshiro said in a low voice as if worried he might set it off with sound alone. "Hexamethylene triperoxide diamine. One of the most unstable chemical explosives on the planet. Especially in the hands of an amateur. Heat fluctuation, friction, the slightest spark could blow the whole thing."

"Which means they can't move it," Jenna interpreted. "They're going to have to either defuse it or blow it on site."

"Any way you put it," Oshiro added, "if your truant schoolboy built more of these babies for Caine, then we're in a heap load of trouble."

CHAPTER 20

THE FIRST THING Morgan noticed was the stench. Fresh vomit. Probably hers. She tried to blink, but all she managed was to peel her eyelids back far enough to trigger a wave of vertigo. She quickly closed them again.

How long had she been out? Probably not too long—Clint's formulas hit fast but didn't usually last longer than an hour or so; they always ended with a wicked hangover. When she was growing up, she'd been his guinea pig, forced to try each variation, but she had forgotten just how awful the aftereffects were.

Nothing to do but ride it out.

Eyes shut, she took a rapid mental inventory: knives gone, barrettes with their lock picks and shims gone, coat gone and along with it her cell phone, and worst of all, her sunglasses. Could have used them right now—as actual sunglasses. She knew from past experience that as soon as she did open her eyes for good, the slightest bit of light would spike through her skull with the force of a sledgehammer.

That's what she didn't have. What did she have? She was still dressed—yeah for the home team there, as the very idea of Gibson's grimy hands on her body made her want to retch. Also, no new injuries; the damn cable noose was gone; she was sitting on what felt like a fairly old rickety wooden chair, no arms, slats along her back, not very tall, but wide enough that her shoulders hurt with the strain from her arms stretched behind her, wrapping around the outside of the chair...and the zip ties. Tighter now. Legs not restrained. Nice.

Okay, that was her. What else was

going on? She listened carefully, heard heavy breathing from a man—no, make that two men. Micah? She resisted the urge to call to him, ask if he was all right. How stupid was it that she even had that reflex? No way in hell was he all right, and what good would her asking do except alert their captors that she was awake? Must be the drugs, still muddling her brain.

A creak and rasp filled the air. Some mechanism that needed oiling. She sniffed. Sawdust. Mold. Rotting wood. Burnt something...it wasn't fresh, not like burning wood, more like at the dentist, but no, not organic...metal? Now that was interesting.

She'd run out of reasons to stall and slit her eyes open gingerly. The tiny amount of light slicing between her eyelids and the loose hair that had fallen over her face was still more than enough to threaten to crack her skull apart. She waited for the roaring in her head to settle and tried again. This time the roar was no stronger than standing on a roof during a thunderstorm while holding a lightning rod. Progress.

Her eyes slowly focused. A man—not that kid, Gibson, this was a grown man, broad shoulders, muscles on top of muscles—was hoisting something using a pulley system. She inched her gaze up. Rafters. They were in a barn.

At first the man blocked the view of whatever hung from the pulley, but then he tied it off and stepped aside. It was Micah. Dangling, his toes dragging in sawdust, arms stretched overhead, face etched with pain. Despite all the movies that used that position, she knew for a fact that it was slow torture: first shoulders dislocating, then the chest muscles giving out, leading to eventual suffocation.

It had been one of her father's favorite forms of restraint. Once he hung them like that, no fish lasted very long before surrendering. Not unless they wanted to end it all—which of course, Clint never let them do. When they died, it would be on his terms and at his bidding, no one else's.

Micah's face was blotchy with the

strain, but no fresh bruises or obvious injuries other than a split lip and swollen, bruised cheek. As much as she wanted to keep her eyes on him, she forced herself to look away, keep searching. She slid her gaze sideways and saw a wall for tools, hand-drawn outlines for various hammers and wrenches. Most of the tools were missing, but the few that remained were clean and shiny, well maintained. Not a barn for animals, some kind of workshop.

Explained the sawdust and the metallic smell—burnt machine oil and distressed metal. Which meant...she edged her gaze in the other direction and was rewarded with the sight of a row of saws.

Handheld saws hung from hooks on a pegboard along with a pair of safety goggles hanging from the wrong spot. Then a row of powered equipment. She recognized a band saw and a lathe, wasn't sure what the next two machines were designed for, but finally came a sturdy looking table saw, its circular blade snapped, leaving behind a silhouette like an animal's claw.

She lolled her head forward, peering below the saw with the broken blade. It sat not six feet away from her in a pile of sawdust. She pieced together the story in her mind: convicts, Gibson driving them here, still in restraints—standard handcuff keys wouldn't work with maximum security restraints, and maybe they didn't have time to steal keys from the guards they killed? Whatever went wrong, at least one of them needed his restraints removed and had been idiot enough to try to use the circular saw instead of just picking the locks.

Thank you, God, for the gift of stupidity, she prayed as her gaze caught the glint of broken metal nestled in the sawdust. Shards from the broken saw blade. Perfect for escaping zip ties. And then killing the man preparing to torture Micah.

She began to cough and gag, retching as if she was going to be sick, rocking her body and the chair.

"Looks like your girlfriend's gonna puke again," the man said. Instead of moving toward Morgan, he stepped back, out of range. Vomiting had that effect on people, made controlling the gag reflex a handy skill to have.

Morgan dry-heaved—perfect word for it as she threw her body to the side and toppled her chair so that its back came to rest in the sawdust. As her body writhed, wracked with gagging, her fingers stretched, searching for the bit of metal.

"Do something," Micah pled. "She's going to choke to death."

"Nah, she's fine."

Where was it? Morgan pushed her body along the floor, now actively expelling what little bit of stomach juices she had left. She recoiled forcibly, this time sending her chair skidding back, and was rewarded with the bite of metal against her fingers. She snared the broken saw tooth. It was jagged and sharp, curved at one end, flaked metal at the other, small enough to palm easily.

She rolled her head up, drool escaping down the side of her chin, sawdust now plastered to her hair and face. The man leered down at her from what seemed an impossible distance—the drugs distorting her depth perception.

"Help me," she croaked.

He laughed, and it was not a pleasant sound. It was the kind of laugh that grated nerves and made her lips curl in disgust—a year ago she would have killed him simply to stop the world from ever being forced to hear that laugh.

Now was not a year ago. Now she had a role to play—if she was going to save Micah.

The man moved behind her, bent down, careful not to touch any of her vomit, and lifted both her and the chair back in place, almost without effort. The chair legs smacked the wood floor hard, rattling through her, setting off another wave of pain in her head.

"Who are you?" she gasped even as her fingers rotated the saw blade into position. She made her voice high and frightened, then finished with a cough and a head bob as if she was still too weak to sit up straight on her own.

"Friend of your father's. Pete Kroft." He circled in front of her, leering down.

She blinked in confusion. "My father's here?"

"No. But he sure as hell will be coming back. As long as I have you around, he's going to do exactly what I tell him to."

He obviously did not know Clint as well as he thought. No matter. She strained to raise her head, finally focusing on Micah. She channeled every B-list actress from every B-list thriller she'd ever seen. "Micah! Are you all right? What did he do to you?"

Pete laughed, obviously enjoying his own role. Didn't he realize what happened to the B-list serial killers in the end?

"Let him go, and I'll do whatever you want," Morgan pleaded. She was telling the truth—as long as whatever Pete wanted was to die a painful death.

He didn't take the bait. "Clint told me you were a tough cookie. That you were like us. He even warned me that taking a hostage might not move you at all."

Pulling out a knife—long, thin, with a wicked hook at the end, the kind of knife you'd use to gut a deer—Pete strolled around Micah, stroking him with his blade.

Morgan felt her blood turn to ice as she imagined exactly what she would do to Pete with that knife.

Pete ended his stroll facing her, one arm draped around Micah's waist, swinging him closer, his other hand holding the knife against Micah's ribcage. Not directly over the heart where an amateur would aim, rather slightly below the ribs, angled up where it could do the most damage.

"Clint said you might even kill a hostage. Just to get them out of the equation. Said you didn't like playing by anyone's rules except your own." His smile turned into a sneer. "Said that was why you had to learn a lesson. That I was free to do anything I wanted. As long as it doesn't leave a permanent scar."

Morgan drew herself up. Clint didn't tell Pete any of that, even though it was true. She'd bet it was Gibson. Feeding Pete's fantasies. How long had he been in prison?

"You win." She rocked the chair, trying to appear agitated when really she was whittling down the last bit of zip tie that bound her. "I surrender. I'll do anything you want. Just please don't hurt him."

Pete turned to her in mock surprise. "Surrender? Without a fight? Without any threats? You're not even asking me to let lover boy here go? What's the catch?"

Despite his skepticism, he did exactly what she wanted. As he taunted her, he moved away from Micah and toward Morgan.

"Don't you dare touch her," Micah shouted. He kicked his legs, trying to get enough leverage to strike Pete but ended up only twirling helplessly from his restraints. "What's wrong? Not enough of a man to face someone your own size? Coward."

Pete stopped, made a tsking motion with the knife. "Want to see how much of a man I am? You get to watch everything I'm going to do to your girl." He crouched before Morgan's chair, caressing her hair with his blade. "Pay attention. Because she's never gonna be the same once I'm through with her."

He grabbed her hair in one hand, twisting it so hard the chair tilted onto the two back legs. Perfect position for gravity to help her when she was ready to make her move. His body slithered up hers, between her legs, pressing against her until his face was directly above hers, staring down into her eyes. "Clint said you were still a virgin. Said as far as he knew, you'd never even been kissed."

He slammed his lips against hers. His hand with the knife he kept between them, sliding the blade up and down her sweater. He pulled harder on her hair, forcing a gasp from her, and thrust his tongue into her mouth.

Morgan closed her eyes. He saw that as a sign of surrender and clamped his mouth over hers with bruising force. Her back was arched so far the chair began to teeter. She snapped her wrists outward, breaking the zip ties, and wiggled the fragment of saw blade so that the sharp, hooked end now faced out between her fingers.

Pete deepened the kiss, practically choking her with his tongue, forcing her head back even farther. She relaxed, letting her head roll to the side, freeing herself long enough to take a breath.

He laughed and sheathed his knife, using that hand to squeeze her cheeks and force her to face him again while his other hand twisted her hair with cruel abandon. He was totally off balance, one knee halfway up her thigh, the other foot planted on the floor, holding her weight and the chair upright, still tipped on the back two legs.

She made a small noise, one that he mistook for pleasure as he probed her mouth even farther, his tongue almost gagging her. The movement finally put him right where she wanted him, exposing his throat.

With one swift movement she whipped her hand up and plunged the steel into the back of his neck. Simultaneously, she gnashed her teeth, biting through his flesh, tearing into his tongue and lower lip, shaking her head to do as much damage as possible before she released it.

He made a noise that would have been a scream if not for the blood gushing from his mouth and the fact that most of his tongue was gone. He didn't even remember to grab for the knife as he arched back, fighting to get free of her embrace.

Which only impaled the serrated teeth of the broken blade deeper. She released him, shoved him back, sending her chair to the floor but she rolled her body free before it hit the ground. Now both his hands were flailing at the back of his head, trying to reach the saw blade, as he staggered away from her. His face was contorted with pain and horror, blood flying through the air with every gasp and gurgle.

Morgan spat out his tongue and part of his lip then lunged at him with a snarl. She launched a kick to his groin that dropped him to his knees, followed by another to his gut that lifted him back into the air before he fell facedown to the floor.

She jumped onto his back, grabbing

his hair, twisting his head back at an unnatural angle, ready to tear out his jugular with her teeth, when through the roaring in her head, she heard a voice.

Micah. Shouting. "Morgan. Stop. He's done. Just stop."

Looking up, she saw herself reflected in Micah's expression. He wore the same look of horror her father's victims had when they realized the truth of who Clinton Caine really was: a monster.

"Morgan. It's okay. He's not going to hurt anyone. Just let him go now." He spoke slowly, carefully, as if scared she'd turn on him next.

She felt her hands choking the life from Pete, felt his body go limp beneath hers, and she didn't want to stop. She knew what came next, that delicious rush of power that came from taking a life. God, how she missed that.

But the way Micah looked at her. No. She couldn't do it. Not with him watching. Because his expression had changed. From horror to disappointment. And she couldn't bear that.

She wrenched her hands free and

rolled off Pete's unconscious body. Blood had spewed everywhere: over him, over her, over the floor, walls, ceiling, painting the sawdust crimson.

Pete made small, primal noises of pain as his body shuddered and twitched. He wasn't going anywhere. If he didn't bleed out through his mouth, her blade had most likely pierced his spinal cord. A lethal blow, once he could no longer use his muscles to expand his chest. Same way they killed frogs in grade school biology, only Morgan hadn't perfected her technique on frogs.

Pushing herself to her feet, she stood, grabbed Pete's knife, and approached Micah. "Let me get you down from there."

He nodded wordlessly, his gaze tracking her movement and the knife. "What you did—"

Her ice-cold fury melted into puddles of lonely dismay sloshing through her veins. For the first time, he'd seen her for who she really was, he knew the full truth.

She moved behind him so he

wouldn't see her face. "You're disgusted. It's okay. It's normal."

And normal was something Morgan clearly was not. She climbed onto a sawhorse and cut him down. He bent over, massaging his wrists, then turned to her. She should have just run, slipped out and left him, but she couldn't deny herself one last look.

So she stayed. He lowered both palms to her shoulders then raised them to frame her face, his hands smearing Pete's blood. He leaned his head down until their foreheads touched, his gaze locked with hers.

"What you did. To him." He inhaled, and she braced herself for the worst. "For me. That was the bravest thing I've ever seen."

She waited so long it was painful. Not as painful as the expression on his face. Poor Micah, she hoped he never, ever tried to play poker.

"But..." She prompted.

He hung his head. Looked away—not at Pete's body, barely moving, not at her, anywhere else.

"But nothing." Not his real voice, a suddenly fake one she'd never heard from him before. "We need to get out of here." He was all business, jogging over to where their coats were piled in the corner and searching through his pockets. "Damn, they took our phones. I heard that kid, Gibson, talking while you were drugged. He's crazy. Wants to blow up a bunch of people."

"Where are Gibson and the others?" Now that her adrenaline had ebbed, her tongue felt thick and her mouth parched. Damn drugs.

"I don't know. They said something about that one's brother and meeting your father." He didn't say Pete's name or look in his direction. Instead, he grabbed his coat and shoved the barn door open without waiting for her. It was getting dark outside. The sun set early this time of year. Probably not quite five, she guessed.

She hugged herself, shivering as the cold air blustered through the barn, bringing with it the smell of fresh blood. Her stomach lurched—the drugs still working their way through her system. "Did they say where? Where are they going? Where are the bombs?"

He stood in the doorway; hands braced against the wood timbers silvered by age, looking out into the gathering night, away from her, and shook his head. "No. Nothing."

She lurched across the barn's uneven floor and found her coat—now with straw and mud smearing its pink wool—and pulled it on while his words finally made their way from her ears to the front of her mind. Damn it, she needed to clear her head. She was useless to anyone like this. A smear of blood on her hand caught her eye. Useless for anything except killing.

She wiped it on her coat, too numb to care. Couldn't blame that on the drugs. It was Micah's reaction, the knowledge that if he could, he'd leave her right here, right now with a body on the floor cooling in the winter night. She pushed herself to catch up with him, her teeth chattering as she stepped into the cold night air. "Micah, are you all right? Did they do anything to you while I was knocked out?"

Even in the dark, his pale eyes blazed, but for once she could not read the emotions on his face. There were too many of them, colliding, a hit-and-run conflagration of fear, anger, resentment, disgust...

"No. I'm fine. We need to call the cops."

The wind shifted, spinning around her in a maelstrom that shredded his words, made it hard to breathe, and suddenly she was falling, falling...but Micah didn't catch her.

CHAPTER 21

IT TOOK ALMOST two hours for the bomb squad to examine and render the IED in the school safe. Afterwards, the lead bomb tech came to the command center RV to shed his heavy bomb disposal jacket and helmet and rehydrate after his long hours sweating in the heat of the protective gear.

"What's your call, Olsen?" Liz asked. Jenna inched closer, listening in. Not like she had anything else to do—Andre and Oshiro were analyzing the data from Gibson's gaming console for the third time, but they had nothing new.

"Let's just say, I'd be very happy if this was a one and done."

"Sorry to say, kid has plenty of supplies. His house clear?"

"My team's been through it twice, both with the e-sniffer and the dogs. Even let the city guys give their K-9 a try. It's clean." He hesitated, shifting his helmet to his other hip. "I'd stand my guys down, but..."

"Yeah. I feel the same. This is building to something."

"This kid knows we've limited resources. He wants us chasing our tails, getting tired, frustrated, sloppy. Thanks to the media, he's probably watching our response, learning more about us than we are about him, sad to say."

"Problem with playing defense. We've no choice but to react to whatever card he plays." She straightened, met Jenna's gaze as if she'd known all along that Jenna was eavesdropping. "Good thing not everyone has to play defense, right?"

He followed her gaze, obviously not following her line of thought, then shrugged and left her and Jenna alone.

"Not everyone has to play by the rules, that's what you really mean?" Jenna said. She kept her voice low. Andre and Oshiro were head to head a few feet away.

Liz's eyes went wide. "Of course not, Ms. Galloway. I'm a professional. Would never suggest that any civilian make use of their freedom to take action outside the constraints that law enforcement is bound by. I'm shocked that you would think such a thing."

"Sorry, my bad. But if you weren't an officer of the law, what would you do? Hypothetically speaking, of course."

Liz pivoted to lean against the counter beside Jenna, her back to the men in the rear of the RV. "Well...for starters I might reach out to Clint's daughter. I mean, I didn't get to talk to her for very long, but it was pretty obvious that she knew more than she was saying. And that she was reluctant to become part of the official record. Now..." She raised a hand as Jenna opened her mouth to argue against any deal offered to Morgan. "I'm not saying she won't someday have to answer for anything she might have been involved with in the past. I'm just saying that right here and now, I have my hands full with an active investigation that very clearly has the possibility of severely impacting public safety. I don't have time to open any old cans of worms, so to speak."

Jenna considered that. She almost wished they did have something they could arrest Morgan for. But Liz had a point. Stopping Clint and Gibson and their partners, the brothers Kroft, had to take priority. "I'll give her a call."

"Good. Let me know if there's anything I should know. From any source."

"Will do." Liz moved down the narrow center aisle to join Oshiro and Andre at the back of the RV.

Jenna slid her phone out and dialed Morgan. No answer. A sharp knock came on the command center's door, and she turned to open it.

"We got something," a patrol officer said, his tone unable to mask his excitement. He climbed into the RV and walked past Jenna to hand Liz an evidence bag. "Found it in the kid's locker."

Liz glanced at it then handed it to Oshiro, who immediately got on his phone even as he began typing on a computer.

"What is it?" Andre asked.

"Receipt," the uniformed officer gushed. "Was with a couple of burner phones."

"Thanks," Liz said, opening the RV's rear door and letting a gust of air inside. Jenna shivered and crossed her arms over her chest. The air was clammy as if it was about to rain. Not quite cold enough for snow, not yet.

"But," the officer resisted Liz's hint, "you can track him with that, right? It's got the serial numbers of the other burner phones. One of them has to lead to him."

"We're on it. I'll let you know as soon as we find anything." Liz peered at the young officer's nameplate. "Officer Wentworth. Keep up the good work."

He nodded and left, closing the door against the chill and first splatters of rain.

"To be that young again," Liz sighed even as she turned to Oshiro. Andre stood, giving her his seat at the computer console.

"We were never that young," Oshiro muttered. "Folks like us, we're born old." Then he nodded, held his phone away from his ear, and tapped the speaker on. "Say again."

"We have a confirmed sighting of Caine," a man's voice came from the phone. "And it's at the same area where one of these burner phones is pinging to."

Oshiro and Liz exchanged glances, their eyes going wide with anticipation.

"Where?" Liz asked, already standing.

"The arena. At the Pitt basketball game." There was a pause. "Caller said Caine was accompanied by another male, fits the description of Gibson Radcliffe. Said they were carrying silver fire extinguishers, dressed in fire department uniforms. Should we evacuate the game?"

Liz leaned forward. "We'll call you back in a minute." She hung up. "If we evacuate and they see it, they might trigger the bombs."

"Not to mention the fact that it'd take a helluva lot of time to clear tens of thousands of people."

"Why would Clint target a basketball game?" Jenna asked. "What's he have to gain?"

"No idea, but we can't risk it. We're going to have to coordinate a full EOD response along with an evacuation—the brass is going to love this. Hope you didn't have any plans for the night," Liz said to Oshiro.

Then she nodded to Jenna and Andre. "Thanks for your assistance, but we can't bring civilians along on this one." She pushed the doors open and jumped out of the RV, calling to Olsen, the bomb squad leader, before Jenna could protest.

"Aw, hell," Oshiro said, pushing back from the computer. "There go my brackets."

CHAPTER 22

MORGAN'S EYES FLUTTERED open, and she strained to focus. She was lying on something soft...a couch? And she was inside. Not the barn. A proper house. "What happened?"

"You fainted." Micah's voice came from the haze above her.

"I don't faint."

"Okay, then. You abruptly fell unconscious so quickly that I couldn't stop you from hitting the ground. I carried you in here. Then you passed out again."

Ouch. That explained the sore jaw. And the headache. Stupid drugs. She felt flushed and freezing at the same time. And thirsty. Very, very thirsty. "Water?"

She squinted across the room. Micah crossed her line of sight as he walked into a kitchen. Between the kitchen and the living room where she sat on a couch covered in roses bigger than a plate was a formal dining room. The table was littered with dirty dishes and soggy, grease-stained pizza boxes and carry-out bags.

Micah reappeared, carrying a bottle of water. He sat beside Morgan, supporting her as she drank eagerly. She choked and sputtered as she gulped it down but couldn't help herself, it felt so good, she was so damn thirsty. He took the bottle from her until her coughing stopped. He stroked the back of her neck with a damp cloth.

"You're burning up. Maybe we should take you to a hospital?"

She shook her head and immediately regretted it. "No. I'll be fine. Clint likes to mix MDMA in with his rohypnol and ketamine. Just a bit dehydrated."

"MDMA—as in Ecstasy? And

Rohypnol, that's the date rape drug, right?" He sounded aghast, as if being drugged was the worst thing that had happened to either of them today.

Morgan looked around, searching for a clock. Had she passed out again? Felt like she'd missed something Micah said, but she wasn't sure. "What time is it? How long was I out?"

"Almost six o'clock. And which time?"

She blinked, her question already half-forgotten in the fog that consumed her. She smacked her lips: they felt dry and chapped. Then she noticed the blood on her hands. A rush of memory stampeded over her.

"The barn...you were...I...I...killed—
" Regret overwhelmed her as she remembered the look on his face when she'd killed Pete. "You saw. You saw me..."

He nodded, his expression grim. "It's okay. Just drink. Everything will be okay. The landline's disconnected, and that man...his phone, he landed on it when he hit the ground. It's dead."

That spiked through her confusion. "Are we safe? Did you clear the house? Check to see that there's no one else here?"

"No. I was taking care of you." He blinked, glanced past her to a staircase. "I'll be right back."

"Wait. I'm coming with you." She staggered to her feet, drawing the knife she'd taken from Pete. Not like he'd be needing it anytime soon. The room swirled, but she hauled in a breath, and it steadied.

"Keep your hand on my elbow," she told him. He thought he was supporting her, but in reality, she wanted to keep track of his movement and stay in front in case they did find anyone.

They found no one. Also, no phones or laptops or any other means of communication, short of emptying a few tins of baked beans and tying the cans together. A bunch of dirty laundry, food wrappers leaving a trail from the first floor up to the bedrooms and back again, discarded newspapers, a cache of weapons—Morgan selected a folding knife to replace her Kershaw and felt better once she slid it into her boot. She also took a 9mm semiautomatic pistol after making sure the magazine was full. Debated on grabbing one of the long guns—there was a nice shotgun—but Micah pulled her away. "That's evidence. We shouldn't touch it."

Like they were going to call the police. She'd made sure she hadn't touched anything that she wasn't taking with her—other than the broken saw blade she'd left behind in Pete's neck. Her DNA was all over him as well. Damn. There had to be some kerosene or gas around, she could douse the corpse and burn it. The house as well, since Micah hadn't been as careful as she'd been...

"Morgan?" Micah was talking, and somehow they'd made it back down to the dining room. She glanced up at him. "Did you hear me? I said we need to go get the cops."

She rummaged through the papers on the table. Nothing that told her where Clint was or when he'd be coming back. She debated waiting, setting a trap for him, Gibson, and Pete's brother. But what to do with Micah?

"You need to go," she told him. "I'll take care of things here."

The bought her a frown. "No. I'm not leaving you. We need to tell the police about that kid and his bombs. And the man in the barn. And we need to get you to a doctor."

She waved his concerns away and tried appealing to his self-interest. "Micah, you're still on probation. If the cops know you were here, they'll send you back to jail."

"They can't do that. We're the victims."

"Until I killed a man." She blew her breath out. He wouldn't leave her, she realized. Best to leave together, and she could grab a car, come back on her own. "Okay, let's go. We'll figure it out on the way."

He followed her out to the car. It was fully dark now, clouds scudding thick and low across the sky, the scent of snow in the air.

Even though he held the door open

for her just like he always did, she noticed that he took care not to stand too close, and he didn't touch her or help her into her seat like usual. In fact, he hadn't really touched her at all, not since she woke.

She settled herself into the passenger seat, pulling her coat tighter, shivering as he climbed in and started the car.

"That guy was going to rape you. It was self-defense." He leaned forward, squinting through the windshield as they reached the end of the drive. Finally, he turned left. "And the drugs. They made you go crazy, lose yourself. Ketamine, that's Special K on the street, causes psychosis, right?"

"It wasn't the drugs. I didn't lose myself. And I wasn't defending myself."

"What? Sure you were." Doubt tainted his voice.

"Micah." His name was a sigh that left an empty ache in its wake. "I was absolutely myself. The purest, truest part of myself. I was defending you. I killed him to save you. It didn't matter what happened to me. But he would have killed you—slowly, painfully. I couldn't let that happen."

He was silent for a long moment. Too long. "What he said, about you killing a hostage to take them out of the equation—"

"I took him out of the equation, instead."

"But if you had to, you would have, you could have—"

How to explain it? "I could have, I would have—past tense. Not now. Not with you."

"Because I'm special, but anyone else is cannon fodder?" His frustration mirrored her own, except his was also charged with the aftershock of almost dying.

"No, no." Was he purposefully twisting her words to make it easier for him to leave her? "That's not what I meant. I meant—what I'm trying to say—I'm not that person anymore."

"Earlier you said you were. Said I shouldn't be with you. Morgan, you practically tore that guy's face off. With your bare teeth."

Some would find that a useful talent in a significant other. The thought raced through her mind, accompanied by a wave of hysteria. Damn drugs still clouding things exactly when she needed to make herself clear.

"I don't want to be that person anymore. Because of you. I'm trying not to be that person anymore." She spread her arms wide. Leaving herself open, vulnerable. "Because of you."

His silence filled the car louder than any words could.

"Thank you," he finally said, surprising her. But also making her wince at the ice in his voice. Distant ice, from another galaxy, beyond the visible stars. "You saved my life. Thank you."

She waited, but he didn't say anything else. City lights came into view as they crested a hill and reached route 22. They didn't have long, and she wasn't sure she'd ever have the chance to see him again, to tell him what was really in her heart—but no, after what he'd been through, what he'd seen, this had to be about him, not her.

She could handle it, she always had.

"You should take some time. I know a guy, Nick Callahan. He's real good to talk to about stuff like this. You can tell him anything."

"How? Without getting you arrested or in worse trouble than you already are?"

"You don't have to worry about me. Seriously. You need to take care of yourself. And then," she hauled in her breath, tamping down her hopes and fears, "then, if you want, we can talk. Maybe even try again."

She spotted the turn for the mall. "Just drop me off—" Then she saw the spotlights arcing over the parking lot and the neon letters announcing the March Madness special event.

"Turn. Turn here." She reached to yank the wheel, but he was already obeying her. "I'm an idiot. This is it. This is Gibson's target. Drop me off. I need to find a phone, call Jenna and Andre. I need to find Gibson. I need to stop—" She clamped her palm over her mouth, looked at Micah in dismay.

"Your father," he finished for her as he steered the Ford into a parking spot. "We need to stop him and Gibson and those bombs."

As much as Morgan despised his choice of pronouns, there was no time to argue.

CHAPTER 23

THE MALL WAS a nightmare of chaos. Sound reverberated from the concrete, glass, and steel across two levels of shopping, echoing through the atrium that connected the upper floor with the lower one. When Morgan and Micah rushed inside, she felt physically repulsed by the crowd pulsating with its jungle beat, a wave of nausea overcoming her for a moment.

Large screen TVs were everywhere, showing commercials now, but as soon as the Pitt game began, they would switch over to live coverage. That way, shoppers could watch as they browsed, ate, and bought, bought, bought.

It was a family affair with free child care in the play area, a basketball court had been set up on the level below the food court with boys lined up to play winners, green screen backdrops with custom computerized settings for the family portrait sittings, and festive pop-up kiosks selling everything from personalized toys to a booth where parents could record bedtime stories.

Micah was her anchor, guiding her through the swarm to the mall directory.

"The security office." He pointed to a square on the map. Security was on the lower level, tucked into the area behind the stairs leading up to the food court. "They'll know what to do."

She didn't share his faith in mall cops. "Go," she told him, leaning against the column that held the map as if she might be sick.

She tried to tell herself she was only acting, although the bright lights and noise kept messing with her balance, making her nauseated. But it wasn't any physical symptoms that kept her from joining Micah. This pain went much, much deeper. "I'll catch up." He turned to leave but she called him back. "Micah."

"What?" And for a moment he was that boy she'd first met—the one who seemed to know her heart without knowing her at all, the one she'd dared trust with her truth. The boy she'd met before she'd ruined everything.

"You should stay there with them. Security. You know what Gibson looks like. Scan all the cameras. Wait for the cops."

He frowned. "You're coming, right?"

"I'll be right behind you." She pressed one arm against her belly. "Hurry."

He waited a beat, searching her face, then nodded and left. She closed her eyes for a brief moment, blocking out the noise and people, and took a breath. He'd be safe, locked away in the security office. Last place Clint would go. First place the cops would.

She opened her eyes, focused, ready. What was Clint's game? Why was he here when he should be miles away, cementing his escape?

Because he *was* here, she knew it. She wasn't sure how she knew—maybe the creeping that crawled below her skin, maybe a subliminal scent only a fellow predator could detect—but Clint was here.

What did he want? She scanned the directory, looking for likely targets. No. What did he *need*? That answer was easy. There were only two things Clint needed to help him reclaim his life: Morgan and money.

Which meant he was going to use Gibson's bombs and the crowd as a diversion. The mall had several branches of banks, but they would all be closed for the day. The electronics store? No, not much cash there, they'd mainly deal in credit cards. Ahh...there. Two jewelry stores, one up here on the main level, one on the opposite end of the mall on the lower level. One of the stores had to be his target—but which one?

———•———

IT WAS AMAZING to see how quickly the first responders cleared out from the high school to head downtown and aid in the efforts at the Pitt game. Jenna watched their flashing lights fade from sight in her rearview mirror as she and Andre drove toward the Radcliffe house to update their client.

"It's hard, isn't it?" Andre said. "Part of you wants to be with them, right in the thick of things."

"Yeah. Until I remember just how awful it can be. A crowd that size, no reliable intel, they have no idea where to send people to keep them safe or even if just the act of evacuating them will set the bombs off."

"They're trained for this. They'll make it work." Spoken with the certainty of a Marine.

"How much does Diane Radcliffe know about what we've found out about Gibson's activities?" Last thing she needed was a hysterical mother on her hands.

"Know? I've given her the facts.

Understand and accept? Not a whole lot. Even when I showed her the evidence that he'd helped Caine's escape, she wrote it off as a school project or script for a video game he was trying to create."

"Denial. Always the first defense."

"She's pretty fragile. Not sure she has any other defenses left to her. Or any support. She begged me not to say anything to her husband."

"She knows that's impossible, right?" Jenna sighed. It was going to be a long night. She glanced in the rearview once again, wishing she had gone with Oshiro, Liz, and the others. "Still no word from Morgan?"

"Can't get through to her. Or Micah."

Strange. Morgan would ignore a call from Jenna but never from Andre. Her phone rang. Local area code but unfamiliar number. "Maybe that's her." She answered it via the car's speaker.

"Is this Jenna Galloway?" It was a man's voice.

Andre leaned forward. "Micah? Is that you?"

"Mr. Stone? Yes, I was with Morgan, and—" Micah's voice dropped and there was a pause as if he was moving. "So much has happened, I can't even tell you everything, not over the phone, but could you come? The security guards won't listen to me, and we need your help. There's a kid with bombs—"

"Gibson Radcliffe?" Jenna asked.

"Yes. How did you know?"

"Where are you? Put Morgan on."

"We're at the mall. I can't put Morgan on."

"Why not, Micah? What happened?" Andre asked.

The kid sounded shaken to his core—and that said a lot, given how calm and level-headed he'd been when he'd first met Jenna after Morgan had literally pulled him and others out of a burning building.

"I—she—she killed a man. It was self-defense," he added in a rush. "But—"

"No. I get it." Andre glanced at Jenna, but all she could give him was a resigned shrug. "Tell us everything."

Jenna let Andre do the talking as she

sped up, weaving through traffic until she reached the turnoff for the mall.

"Hang on, Micah. We'll be there in two minutes."

CHAPTER 24

ONCE THEY GOT to the mall, Gibson made the rounds, checking his explosive charges while Clint maneuvered into position to grab the diamonds.

Paul waited outside in the getaway car. Poor slob had no idea he was sitting on a bomb that would pretty much incinerate any chance of identifying him— especially since Clint had paid someone to switch their medical records in the prison's computer system. By the time the cops figured out it wasn't Clint's body, Gibson and Clint would be picking up chicks on some island paradise with no extradition treaty.

Gibson had cased their target and knew exactly when the jewelry store's vault would be open, how many guards inside and outside the store, and which display cases had the real stones and not cheap fakes. He'd even taken the time to map out the mall's fire suppression controls, clocked the response time of the guards, and had learned the code to gain entry to the security office that controlled the sprinkler system, fire alarm, and electronic locks on the mall's doors.

Clint was going to be so proud of him by the time tonight was over—he'd forget all about Morgan, leave her behind without wasting a thought. Because Gibson wasn't just giving Clint a diversion, he was creating a spectacle.

Clint's plan was simple, so simple that Gibson couldn't resist improving on it. While the cops were chasing the false bomb scare downtown, the real bombs were here at the mall. All Clint had asked for was some smoke bombs and a few firecrackers to draw out the security guards and create enough of a panic that he could grab the diamonds.

Paul had hogged all their premium ingredients to make the bombs his brother had delivered to the Pitt game—said even if they weren't going to be detonated, they had to be real enough to keep the cops tied up. But Gibson had still been able to improvise three pipe bombs that would do the job nicely.

Clint wanted smoke and noise, he was going to get it, along with screams and blood and terror-fueled panic that would cloak their escape. He'd see for himself that Gibson was a far greater and more dangerous predator than pretty little Morgan ever was or could be.

Gibson was on the lower level in the center of the atrium, watching the pretty families getting their pretty pictures taken in front of a fake green screen. Only thing missing was his family. Damn. He'd really wanted them here for the main event. Oh, to see the look on his stepdad's face when he realized it was Gibson with all the power...

The large screens flicked away from the mall commercials and switched to a countdown to the start of the game. A countdown Gibson and Clint were using to coordinate the start of their own game.

Most of the men in the place stopped to stare at the nearest screen while the women consulted their promo flyers for the special sales for each period and discount codes triggered by Pitt's score at specific times.

Too bad none of them were going to be around to take advantage of any of the March Madness, Gibson thought with a smile, his finger on his phone, ready to detonate the first wave. Ten, nine, eight...

———•———

MORGAN PUSHED THROUGH the crowds of shoppers who stood between her and the jewelry store. As she moved, she ran through scenarios in her head. Clint wouldn't plant bombs in the store—it would risk scattering the jewels or burying them under rubble, not to mention the danger to himself if Gibson miscalculated the strength of the charge or placed it in the wrong area.

So, no bomb in the store. Which meant she'd have to leave Gibson and finding the charges in Micah's hands. Focus on Clint. How to rob a jewelry store during the chaos of a bombing?

The store would go into lockdown. There'd be guards inside along with any customers caught in the store. But the store would also have its own rear exit— no way did they bring shipments of precious gems through the mall. Which meant Clint had to be inside the store when the bomb went off. All she had to do was either be there with him or stop him before he could get inside.

She quickened her pace, keeping to the railing overlooking the atrium. Fewer people there, away from the storefronts, and it positioned her with a better sight line. She scanned the area between her and the jewelry store on the other side of the food court. No sign of Clint, but she couldn't see inside the store itself. Was she too late?

The large screen TVs over the atrium beside her switched from a commercial to a neon-bright animated countdown. The game was about to start.

Morgan entered the food court, now had a direct line of sight into the jewelry store. No Clint. But a man was approaching from the stairs leading up from the atrium. His face was turned away from her, he was average height, average weight, and the way he moved...Clint, it had to be.

No way could she reach him in time. She raised her pistol. "Clint!"

All eyes turned to her as she marched toward the man. Several people in the food court yelled, mostly women calling their children to them, backing away from the crazy girl with the gun and the bloodstained coat. In her periphery, she spotted a few men actually step toward her, ready to play hero, but they quickly thought the better of it—smart men.

"Everyone, get out. Now." She fired her gun into the roof to make her point. They scattered toward the mall exit behind her.

Clint paused, only long enough to

twist a glance in her direction. Then he shifted his gaze to the atrium with its countdown clock. He turned and sprinted toward the store.

No luck. Morgan's gunshot and the crowd's shouts had alerted the store's guards. Two now stood inside the entrance, the door sliding shut, locking Clint out.

He whirled. Before she could reach him, he vanished back down the staircase to the lower level.

Morgan took a step, following, when the countdown hit one and the world shattered around her in a blaze of flame, smoke, and screams.

———•———

JENNA AND ANDRE rushed into the mall through the lower level entrance.

"Micah said he was in the security office," Andre said, scanning the mall directory.

"You go meet him, I'll keep an eye out for Gibson," she told him. "If you spot anything on the cameras, you can direct me there." She tapped her earbud.

"Got it." He headed toward the office beneath the steps leading up to the main level.

She searched the crowd, most of them mesmerized by the computerized countdown on the screens above them. How the hell were they going to find one kid in this madhouse?

A shot sounded from the upper level. She looked up—amazed that so many of the people around her didn't. Did they think it was a sound effect?—and spotted Morgan heading past the food court, aiming a weapon at someone out of sight.

"Andre," she said into her microphone. "Upper level. Morgan's found someone."

"I'm on it."

Before she could answer, she noticed a bright silver fire extinguisher sitting at the base of a pop-up kiosk selling organic soy candles. Kind of made sense, except...none of the candles were actually lit. She ran to the kiosk where the vendor was talking with a single customer. "Is that your fire extinguisher?"

He frowned at her interruption, but the urgency in her tone caught his attention. "No. It was here when I opened. Figured it was some kind of safety rule."

"Get out. Now." They hesitated. "Federal agent," she lied. "Evacuate the area. Now!" The customer fled, and the salesman grabbed his cash box and followed.

Jenna scanned the area, looking for the closest fire alarm. There, on the wall near the AED station. She raced for it, had just pulled it, when a blast sent her reeling off her feet, her ears filling with pressure, muffling the sound, but there was no mistaking the flames shooting out in all directions from where the candle kiosk had stood moments before.

Footsteps and shrieks thundered through the floor—she shook her head; how had she gotten to the floor?—people ran past, clutching bags and children and phones.

Another explosion shook the building, this one farther down at the other end of the mall—or maybe it was the ringing in her ears making it sound that way. Jenna scrambled to her feet, fell again as someone shoved past her, then finally an anonymous Good Samaritan helped her back up. She lost him in the crowd as she blinked to clear her vision and tried to find Andre. He'd been on the stairs to the upper level, but she couldn't see him through the throng of people.

"Andre!" she shouted. Then she realized she'd lost her earpiece. No way could anyone hear her over the stampede. She pushed her way toward the stairs. Smoke billowed from both ends of the mall.

A groaning noise, louder than the alarms, screams, and ringing in her ears came from above her. She glanced back just as one of the large screen monitors broke free of its cable and fell, landing in the middle of what had been, a minute ago, the children's play area.

The crowd moved fast, quickly emptying, except for the wounded and those tending to them. She'd almost made it to the center of the atrium when she spotted a man moving slowly, turning in a circle, observing the chaos, a ghastly smile playing across his face.

Gibson Radcliffe.

CHAPTER 25

THE RAILING OVERLOOKING the atrium kept Morgan on her feet as the two blasts shook the building. The lights flickered but then steadied, alarms blared, and one of the large monitors crashed to the ground below.

She ignored it all as she continued across the now-empty food court toward the last place she'd seen Clint at the top of the steps. Her head throbbed, and her balance and hearing weren't cooperating with each other, but she wasn't about to let him get away. Not this time.

Clint appeared at the top of the

stairs. Holding a gun on Andre. What the hell was Andre doing here? She didn't have time to come up with an answer as she skidded to a stop and raised her pistol. "Andre, down!"

Then Clint showed her his other hand. The one with the dead man's trigger and a suicide vest bristling with explosives. "Stop right there or he dies."

"You mean you both die."

"Fine with me, little girl. One more step, and I'll kill us all."

Morgan stopped. She was about fifteen feet away, only three tables between her and Andre. The blare of the alarms continued, but it was as if her hearing and vision had narrowed to a focused cone; she had no problem hearing Clint.

"Let him go," she yelled across the empty space.

"Why should I?" Clint answered amicably. As if they had all the time in the world.

She hoped that meant that he and Gibson had no more bombs ready to go off. She risked a glance over the railing to her left, wasn't all that surprised to see Jenna standing in the atrium, holding a weapon on Gibson.

"Tell you what," Clint continued, mistaking her hesitation for weakness. "You come join us, and I'll keep him alive. We'll all leave together."

Andre shook his head despite Clint jamming the pistol into his cheek. She remembered what Pete had said back in the cabin before she tore his face apart. He'd said she'd kill a hostage before she let them be used against her.

She moved her aim from Clint to Andre, surprised her pistol wasn't shaking. The rest of her felt as if it was, shaking so hard she had to blink back tears. Then she lowered the gun, her arm dropping uselessly to her side. "Take me instead."

Clint's laughter was as wicked as she remembered. "Interesting. You'd leave all these people to die, just to save one man?"

Jenna could handle Gibson. No one else would die here. Not tonight. But Clint didn't need to know that.

"Let him go. Take me instead." She set her pistol on the table beside her, raised her hands.

"Why would you do that?" He sounded genuinely interested. "You know what I'm going to do to you, the price of betrayal."

"I know. But he's family."

The look of confusion and resentment that twisted Clint's face was worth all the diamonds she'd prevented him from stealing. Even more priceless was the smile Andre gave her. A smile that stopped her shaking and helped thaw the icy fist that gripped her. No one had ever looked at her that way before, not even Micah. More than grateful or thankful. Proud. Loving. As if her treacherous, bloody, deceitful life was actually worth something.

That smile was everything.

Clint considered. "Only if you wear the vest." He handed the vest to Andre and nudged him forward. "Take it to her. She puts it on, you're free to go. Any funny business, and I blow you both up."

Andre slowly walked toward her, his

expression turning thoughtful as he measured his steps. She knew what he was thinking: how far would Clint's detonator reach? Could they dump the vest and run fast enough to escape the explosion? Maybe if he threw it over the side into the courtyard below...his gaze angled that way and a frown filled his face. Too many people, including Jenna.

In the end, he stopped halfway between them and slid the vest on, snapping the padlock that secured it shut.

"Andre, no!" Vest or no vest, she rushed to him.

"Only way." His voice was low, for her ears alone. "Tell Jenna—"

"She knows." Lock picks, she needed lock picks. Damn it. She'd lost her barrettes, her sunglasses, anything useful. "Why—"

"You know why. I'm sorry no one's told you before now. It shouldn't be this way. You deserve better, Morgan."

She blinked hard against tears. She didn't cry, she reminded herself. She never cried. "I don't understand."

He was backing away, almost to

Clint. "Because you're family. And you're worth it." Clint grabbed him by the arm. "Never forget that, Morgan Ames."

Clint pulled him to the stairs. Morgan reached for her gun, but who was she going to shoot? Not Clint or he'd use the dead man's switch to kill them all.

Andre? It would be the humane thing to do, spare him whatever Clint had planned. She squeezed one eye shut, trying to lock in her aim, but her hand was trembling. Once again, she lowered the weapon in defeat. God help her, she couldn't do it. She couldn't take the shot.

They vanished down the stairs, and the world returned in a rush of noise so furious she staggered against the railing, fighting to remain upright. She watched Clint push Andre before him toward the exit.

Jenna shouted. "Stop!"

Clint whirled, saw Jenna holding her weapon on Gibson, and actually laughed. Then he raised his hand with the pistol, aimed, and shot Gibson. He shoved Andre out the exit without looking back.

Gibson staggered, grabbing his arm.

Morgan was surprised Clint had hit him at all, given the distance and distractions. Gibson shouted Clint's name. But it was too late. Clint and Andre were gone.

Jenna ran toward the exit, following Clint and Andre.

"Jenna, no!"

"It should have been you," Jenna shouted back, her voice choked with smoke and fury.

Morgan kept her sights on Gibson. She couldn't shoot him, not if he still had his own dead man's switch. Besides, there were too many people on the lower level, most of them wounded. He jerked his head up at Jenna's sudden departure, glanced around in surprise as if not sure what to do next.

Still clutching his arm, Gibson scuttled to a spot immediately below Morgan, crossing into her blind spot.

Suddenly she knew where he was headed—the last place anyone would look for a mad bomber while the place was being evacuated and the one place where he had control of everything, from the alarms to the locks to the sprinkler system: the security office.

Exactly where she'd sent Micah to wait.

CHAPTER 26

MORGAN WAS TORN. Gibson was heading right toward Micah, but Clint was escaping with Andre. Trusting Jenna to follow Clint and Andre—as much as she hated that option, she knew Jenna would never endanger Andre—Morgan raced down the stairs.

As she arrived on the lower floor, the fire sprinklers finally activated, adding the pounding water to the smoke and confusion. She turned away from the atrium and headed back beneath the stairs to the security office. The door was ajar, although the keypad was blinking red. Pistol in hand, she burst into the office.

It was empty. Except for Micah, his face cast in stark shadow by the glow of the monitors surrounding him, standing over Gibson. Micah's hand was raised, fist ready to strike, as he whirled to face Morgan. Gibson cowered beneath the monitors, both hands trying to stop his nose from bleeding, his one arm also smeared with blood.

"Clint shot me," he moaned. "He left me behind." His cocky smile was gone; he seemed shaken as much by Clint's betrayal as from his wounds.

Her gaze went from one to the other then back to Micah. "Nice work."

"He had this—I think he was going to blow up Andre and Clint." He handed her a cell phone. "Or maybe more bombs."

"He deserved it. He betrayed me," Gibson muttered, his eyes glazed, the whites showing all around.

Micah crouched and quickly searched Gibson, removing everything from his pockets. Morgan didn't help, she was too busy scanning the monitors for signs of Clint and Andre.

"I saw what you did," Micah said, his tone tentative. "Were you really going to wear that vest? Go with your father to save Andre?"

"Yes." She spotted Jenna weaving through the crowd streaming out of the mall, followed her through the cameras as she left the throng behind and began to make her way through the parked cars. Emergency response vehicles were rolling in, their lights strobing in the grainy security footage, making it difficult to see.

"Why? Was it because you knew your father wouldn't actually hurt you?"

She understood that he needed to make sense of everything that happened today. It would be quicker to give him a lie that served as an easy answer. But she couldn't. "No. Clint would hurt me. He would kill me. But he'll do worse to Andre if I can't stop him."

Micah stood at her side, flipping through more of the cameras. "Why does he hate Andre so much?"

"He doesn't." She spotted movement at the far end of the employee lot. "He doesn't even know Andre. He'd hurt him to hurt me."

"Because he hates you that much?" Confusion clouded his voice. Micah had two loving mothers, was wanted and cherished. Her world was as foreign as life on Mars to someone like him.

She zoomed in on the camera. Two men skirting the shadows. Had to be Clint and Andre. "No. Because he wants me that much. To Clint that's the same as love. And hate." She shrugged. "Don't try to make sense of it." She noted the parking row Clint turned down and turned to leave. "You okay watching Gibson? The cops will be here soon, and the fire doesn't seem to be spreading."

Micah nodded. "Go. I have this." Before she could move he startled her by grasping her elbows. Then he did something she totally did not understand—but wished with all her might that she did. He leaned forward and kissed her gently on the forehead. "When this is over, come find me."

No idea how to respond, she did what came natural. She shoved her confusion aside, turned, and ran.

———•———

JENNA RACED THROUGH the parking lot, heading to the rear of the mall where employees left their cars. Clint would never risk getting caught in the maelstrom of panicked shoppers escaping Gibson's firebombs, he'd make sure his escape route was clear. As she circled around the corner, she spotted movement at the end of the row of cars, near the exit from the lot. A silver SUV with tinted windows. Light from an open door illuminated a man for a split second on the passenger side of the vehicle. Clint. But where was Andre? Already in the SUV? The door slammed shut and the light went out.

"Stop and show me your hands," she shouted as she ran toward Clint, keeping several cars between them for cover.

"Don't come any closer," he yelled back, turning to face her. He raised his hand high so she could see he wasn't holding a gun. Rather he held some kind of detonator. "I mean it. I'll blow it all sky high."

Did he have control of the explosives in the mall, not Gibson? She hesitated. Could she risk it? But he was so close, and she couldn't let him take Andre as hostage. She skirted the next car, still heading toward Clint.

"Drop it," she called out.

He laughed. "I really don't think you want me to do that. I'll end us both before I go back to prison."

She couldn't shoot him, not if the detonator had a dead man's switch. But she also couldn't let him go—not when he could still blow up the mall or kill Andre. She kept her pistol aimed on him.

"I'll kill myself and your partner. You know I'll do it, Jenna."

She hated that he knew her name. The way he said it made her cringe, not only in revulsion, but in remembered fear. Fear of when he'd held her captive. Not this time. She wasn't his victim. She was the one who was going to stop him once and for all, end this and save Andre.

She steeled her will and her voice. "Deactivate the device and put your hands up."

For a moment she thought he was going to comply. He sidled away from the vehicle, raising both hands. But then he spun and flung himself to the ground.

Before Jenna could react, the world exploded in a blast of noise and a rush of wind that knocked her off her feet. Car alarms shrieked all around her—the only sound that could pierce the ringing in her ears. Flaming debris fell from the sky, bouncing from the pavement that she swore was still moving beneath her.

Hands grabbed her and pulled her along the blacktop, away from the flames, and then hauled her to her feet.

"You okay?" someone shouted. Jenna blinked and Morgan's face came into focus. But she didn't care about Morgan. Andre. Where was Andre? She stumbled, turning around, and found herself staring into a maw of black, oily smoke and flames. The SUV. Clint had blown up the SUV. He'd been standing right there—had he killed himself along with Andre?

"Andre!" Jenna screamed even though she couldn't hear her own voice. She lunged toward the blazing car, but Morgan tackled her. They both ended up on the pavement.

"No," Jenna sobbed. But even she could see that no one could have survived the explosion. "No."

Clint warned her. Told her what he'd do. And now Andre was dead, and it was all her fault.

Morgan was hugging her, holding her in place as if worried that Jenna would try to leap into the flames. Jenna turned in her embrace, pushing back to give herself room. She raised a hand, used it to wipe her tears, surprised that it came away streaked with blood and mucus, and stared at it for a long moment. Then she stared at Morgan.

It wasn't Jenna's fault that Andre was dead.

She slapped Morgan so hard her hand stung with the blow. Morgan, for the only time since Jenna had met her, was caught off-guard, the slap rocking her back against the car behind her. Her eyes blazed, the whites showing around her dark pupils, and she held one hand to her cheek. Then, without saying a word, she climbed to her feet.

"Where are you going?" Jenna spat the words with all the venom and pain that pulsed through her veins. Somehow she was standing as well, even though she didn't remember exactly how she'd gotten there.

Morgan's gaze raked the parking lot, ignoring the burning SUV. "I'm going to find Clint. I'm going to find him, and then I'm going to kill him."

"You idiot!" Jenna was screaming and didn't care. "Clint's dead—he just blew himself up, along with Andre."

Morgan frowned. Uncertainty danced across her face. Jenna might have even enjoyed seeing her flustered if the circumstances had been different.

"No," Morgan said slowly. "No. He wouldn't kill himself."

"He would if the alternative was going back to prison. He's dead. And he took Andre with him."

"Maybe..." She shook her head. "No. We need to find the truth."

She walked away, vanishing into the smoke. Leaving Jenna alone.

CHAPTER 27

MORGAN HEADED BACK toward the mall, but a cordon of local police were controlling the entrance, guarding the first responders who were getting the wounded out. She fell back, using the anonymity of the crowd, pausing only to lift a cell phone from one of the unsuspecting gawkers.

She dialed Micah. He answered just as Jenna arrived, favoring Morgan with a death glare.

"Micah, ask Gibson if there are any more bombs," she said, putting the phone on speaker and holding it so Jenna could hear above the sound of the crowd and the fire trucks.

"He says no."

"What about at the arena?" Jenna put in.

There was another pause. "He says those are a diversion. Says the plan was for him and Clint to leave together, Clint was going to have Gibson wear the suicide vest in case anyone tried to stop them."

A glimmer of hope crossed Jenna's face. "So the vest was a fake?"

A longer pause. "No. He says it was real. Just in case Clint had to take someone inside the store hostage."

"Right out of the Kroft brothers' playbook," Jenna muttered. "So he and Clint were going to escape in the SUV?"

"No." This time it was Gibson's voice. He sounded eager to help—made her wonder how Micah had accomplished that. But not too surprised. Micah was a good listener. "The SUV is rigged to blow. Clint's plan was to kill one of the brothers in the explosion, the cops would think it was him, give us time to run."

Morgan met Jenna's gaze. "There's

another car."

"There's another car," Jenna repeated the words as a prayer. She turned to the phone. "Gibson. What car did Clint take? Where would he go?"

"Silver Toyota. I don't know where he's headed." Gibson's tone turned spiteful. "But do me a favor, and when you find him, put a bullet through his head."

Jenna clenched her jaw. "Micah, stay put. There's going to be a lot of people who want to talk to you and Gibson. Just tell them what you told us."

"Where are you and Morgan going?" Micah asked.

"Not sure yet, but we'll let you know once we figure it out." Jenna hung up before Morgan could say anything. "So. Where are we going?"

"You weren't invited." Last thing Morgan needed was Jenna slowing her down—or worse, rushing in and forcing Clint's hand.

"Hell I wasn't."

Morgan didn't have time for Jenna's theatrics. "I can't save Andre if I'm watching out for you as well."

"Like I'd trust you to watch my back. Besides, this isn't about you or me coming back alive. It's about Andre. Period."

"So if it comes down to a choice..." Morgan already knew who she'd choose, and she already knew who Jenna would choose. The hard one to convince would be Andre. His stubborn heroics were what had gotten them into this to start with. No matter that he'd been saving Morgan's life at the time...in fact, that only made things worse. He was a good man, deserved so much better than what life had thrown at him—and yet, he'd been willing to sacrifice it all for her.

She couldn't rest, not with that burden weighing her down. From the haunted look in Jenna's eyes, Jenna felt the same.

"If it comes down to it, we knock him out, do what needs to be done, and drag him out of there. You good with that?" Jenna asked.

"Absolutely. Where's your car?"

Jenna led her through the parking lot, skirting the crowd and the first responders. Straggling lines of cars converged at the main exits, people fleeing the scene and caught in a massive traffic jam. "Damn, this will take all night."

"Follow me." Morgan led the way on foot past the snarled traffic.

They crossed a strip of trees that separated the mall from one of the smaller shopping areas ringing it and then sprinted to the far side of the shopping center where there was a popular all night bowling pub. A few people stood outside, gawking at the lights and smoke, but no one was paying any attention to the cars.

Since she had none of her usual tools—including her phone with its universal electronic vehicle access program—their selection was limited. As Morgan decided on an older but well-maintained minivan, Jenna's phone rang.

"It's Andre," she said eagerly. As if she thought Andre had overpowered Clint and escaped his custody. Morgan started to caution her, but too late, Jenna answered it. "Andre?"

"No, Jenna. I'm afraid Mr. Stone is a

bit indisposed at the moment."

"If you hurt him—" It was an empty threat and they all knew it.

Clint chuckled. "You have something I want, I have something you want. Let's make a deal." He said the last in the overblown tones of a game show host. "I'll give you your precious Mr. Stone in exchange for a hundred thousand dollars and my daughter."

"Done," Jenna said before Morgan could protest. "When and where?"

"Midnight. Site of Morgan's first kill. She'll tell you how to get there."

"That's not much time—"

"Midnight. A minute late, a dollar short, any sign of the cops, and you'll be scraping Mr. Stone into a pudding cup—or rather, what's left of him. I hear suicide bombers often have much of their body vaporized by the force of the blast."

He hung up. Jenna turned to Morgan. "Where are we going? Site of your first kill? Where's that?"

Her words were a staccato jumble, sparked by hope. Hope was the opposite of what Morgan felt. She felt drained, empty of any emotion.

"When Clint first took me," she said, wrapping her arms around her as rain began to fall. "He took me to a remote cabin. Up on Tussey Mountain. Taught me how to stalk prey. Survival skills. But first he made me kill animals he caught and staked out for me."

"Boohoo for you. Where, Morgan? Tell me where?"

"It's no good. You'll never stop him or catch him. Not there. He knows those mountains, knows the trails, knows where to find cover."

"I don't care about catching him. I just want Andre back. Alive."

Morgan's chest heaved as her sigh escaped her. "That's what I want, too."

"Then it's settled. You for Andre." Jenna's tone was devoid of emotion.

"I'll take you there. Me for Andre."

"Once he's safe," Jenna offered her words as a consolation prize, "then you can kill Clint. I don't give a damn."

Morgan wished she was half as certain of the outcome. But Jenna was right. Someone was going to die tonight.

As long as it wasn't Andre, she could live
with that.

CHAPTER 28

THE GROWL OF an ATV in the distance announced Clint's arrival. He was late, and Morgan was freezing, standing in the clearing, the snow alternating with sleet and rain to turn the ground to black ice. He'd planned it that way, had wanted the cold to leech all her anger and the strength it gave her.

After Jenna had gathered what cash she could, they'd switched cars and headed toward the mountain, arriving as early as possible. All Morgan had asked for in exchange for her cooperation was a quick stop to torch Pete's body and the barn and that Jenna make sure Micah received the reward money. Jenna didn't care about money, although she would enjoy the prestige of collecting the bounties on the Kroft brothers as well as Clint, so she'd readily agreed.

Clint had called with more specific instructions after they left their car at the end of the last stretch of drivable road. Logging trail was more like it. Thankfully, it was cold enough that the mud was frozen solid, making it passable.

At least he'd let Morgan wear her coat—that and her underwear and a pair of flats. He knew her too well, knew her proclivity to squirrel weapons wherever she could. But she also knew him, knew he would use any excuse, even an imaginary one, to renege on his word.

She'd refused to wear an earbud, despite the comfort it would have given her, hearing the others. No. She'd come as Clint instructed: naked and alone.

Also as instructed, as she waited, she held the canvas gym bag Jenna had given her. She ran through the various scenarios one last time. Most of them did not end well for Morgan. It didn't matter. Nothing mattered. As long as they got Andre back.

Morgan craned her neck and looked up, stretching. The rain had finally stopped, the clouds shredded by the wind, unveiling a canopy of black ink sparking with more stars than she'd ever seen before. When she looked back down at her feet, the wet, black mud had been transformed into a mirror, and it was as if she stood on the stars themselves.

No matter how bloody the deeds Clint kept her busy at, she'd learned at an early age to search out the magical moments like this one. It felt as if she could stop time—for a short while, at any rate—immerse herself in the miracle of the world she lived in...until Clint yanked her back to his bloody reality.

More than anything, this was how she'd survived those years with Clint. These split-second vanishments where she left her life behind. Nick called it dissociation. Said it was a defense mechanism. Jenna called her frozen moments daydreaming, while Andre would say nothing, merely watch over her, protect her until she came back. Micah said she had the eye of an artist, drawn to beauty. Of course he would say that, he had the soul of a poet. In fact, one of her most cherished vanished moments was when they'd first met.

Clint's arrival silenced the night noises. Shifting her weight to get a better grip on the canvas gym bag in her hands, she turned to face the direction the ATV would come from.

The clearing was at the top of a ridge. To the right, a sheer drop down a granite cliff onto the scraggly deadwood loggers had bulldozed over the edge and left behind to rot.

In front of her was thick forest, hemlocks and rhododendrons, easy to vanish into and escape pursuit if you knew the area. Clint would leave that way, she was certain. Oshiro and Liz Harding had agreed, although they'd stretched their cordon as wide as possible, to cover all options.

It wouldn't work, she'd argued before Jenna had called in

reinforcements. Clint knew this area too well. But Jenna was former law enforcement, placed her faith in protocols and training and operating procedures. After all, Clint was just one man, she'd said. Morgan had been half tempted to grab the cash and do the exchange on her own, but the others hadn't let her out of their sight, so she had no choice.

No, that was a lie. She'd always had a choice. Just this time she was choosing to trust that the others were as determined to save Andre as she was.

Clint came from her left, the ATV's headlight piercing the black night. More forest there, but also a few cabins. And behind her, far behind her, lay the gravel road that led to the two-lane highway and civilization. The forest behind her had been logged more than once, leaving it thinned out, littered with clearings and deadwood, easy to spot anyone approaching.

The ATV paused at the edge of the clearing. She wondered if it would get mired in the mud at her feet but knew she couldn't get that lucky.

The others wanted her to wear a wire and carry a weapon, but for once in her life, Morgan had forsaken weapons. She'd come to this battle naked except for her coat, armed only with her wits and her fists. But after almost an hour standing in the wind and rain waiting for Clint, she was stiff and frozen solid, her mind almost as numb as her body.

"I'm here," she called out. "Just like you asked. No weapons. No cops." She raised the bag, her arms shaking with its weight and the cold. "Just the money. Like you asked."

The ATV's engine revved in reply. "Open your coat, let me see for myself."

Setting the bag at her feet in the mud, she fumbled the buttons open on her coat, the wool now frozen hard, no longer soft and pliable. She slipped it off and circled around, wind slicing into her bare flesh. As soon as she made a full revolution, she quickly retreated into its feeble embrace, the buttons slipping through her numb fingers, going into the wrong holes, but she didn't care, she needed the warmth, any warmth, even if it was merely a faint promise of protecting her from the wicked wind that swept across the clearing.

"Where's Andre?" Her voice wavered as her teeth chattered. "Is he okay?"

"I'm here," came a reply. Andre's voice but choked and a bit blurred as if he were having a difficult time enunciating. From pain or injury, she couldn't be sure. "I'm okay." The last was a lie, she was certain of that.

"Stone will wait here," Clint called.

Morgan jerked at the sound of his voice. Filled with command and certainty, as always. Every fiber of her being yearned to obey—once upon a time, obeying that voice was all that had kept her alive.

But not now, she reminded herself, the thought slicing through the muddle the cold had made of her brain. Never again.

"No. I want to see him." After all, what was to stop Clint from slicing Andre's throat and leaving him to bleed out. "Bring him with you." She raised the bag again. It was getting heavier and heavier. "If you want your money."

No answer for a long moment but then the ATV drove into the clearing. Two men on it: one driving, one draped over the rear storage area like a deer carcass. It stopped just outside of the shadows cast by the forest beyond. The driver shoved the other man off as if he were a bundle of laundry.

"Andre," she shouted.

Andre rolled toward her voice. Finally she could see his face. It was swollen, too dark to see the bruises she knew were there, but he was alive. His wrists and ankles were bound behind him, so all he could do was raise his head. And he still wore the damn vest with the damn bomb.

"Your turn," Clint said. "You and the money are coming with me. No funny business. Or your friend here gets blown to bits." He raised a detonator.

Exactly what they'd expected. Now she just had to play her part while the others rescued Andre. Only flaw in their plan was no one could guarantee that the jammers they'd brought would actually block the signal from the detonator. Which meant everything had to go according to Clint's plan until he and the detonator were either out of range or neutralized.

"Come and get me," she called to Clint. Then she added the one word she knew he could not resist. "Father."

The ATV spun toward her, its headlights blinding. It pulled to a stop before her. Clint was dressed like a hunter in layers of thick camouflage that left him toasty warm, no doubt. Unlike Morgan who could barely move, she was so stiff with the cold.

"Climb on," he ordered.

"First, give me the detonator." No way in hell would she trust him to keep his word and not use it before they were beyond its range.

He scowled at her, his lips twisting into a pout but then handed it over. Her fingers were dead with cold; she could barely wrap them around it, squeezing the button he indicated.

"Don't you drop that, now. The dead

man's switch is live." Clint chuckled at his own pun. He yanked the bag from her other hand—good thing as she was about ready to drop it, it was too heavy—and peered into it. Satisfied by the real cash on top of the dummy bills, he threw it into the ATV's rear compartment.

"Now, you. Get on." He scooted back in his seat, motioning her to sit in front of him.

She climbed on, her movements awkward and slow. He circled one arm around her, holding a knife—a wicked sharp Tanto blade—below the left side of her rib cage, aiming up. Then he began to search her, running his free hand over her coat then her body, checking everywhere.

At one point she slipped, falling forward over the handlebars, barely catching herself against the fender that shielded the front wheels. As she fought to hold onto the detonator, the knife pricked her, just a small cut, a reminder of what was possible in Clint's world.

"Do you remember this place?" he whispered in her ear as his hands did their business. "When I first rescued you, I brought you here. Taught you what life was really about. Shared with you all my secrets."

"I killed my first deer here," she answered, her voice sounding like tin. Flat yet malleable. "Slit its throat. You taught me how to skin and gut it."

"I taught you everything." His tone was a knife edge.

Clint wasn't stupid. He'd be sure to dispose of the bag with its tracker as soon as he stopped long enough to learn that the only cash in it were a few actual bills on top—then their plan was doomed. He'd escape again. And next time when he came for Morgan, he'd be even more furious.

She glanced down, the ice-slicked mud reflecting the sky as if she floated above an ocean of stars, and remembered the daydream—dread-dream was more like it—she'd had at Nick's office yesterday. All of the people she cared for most, they would all be at risk if Clint escaped. Because of her.

"How quickly you forgot everything,"

he continued, sliding his hand down her calf, slipping her shoe off and flinging it to the mud. Then he switched to her other leg. "But we're together again. That's all that matters."

"And my friends?"

His hand froze, hovering above her skin. Mistake, she chided herself. Friends weren't part of Clint's delusion. She held her breath, waiting for his answer.

"You've grown weak without me. Relying on others." He ran his hands through her hair—one of her favorite hiding places for razor blades and lock picks. He found nothing. "I taught you better than that. Family is everything. Family is the only thing."

Once Clint discovered her betrayal, no matter the danger to himself, he would return. Because of her. He would hunt down everyone she loved—could she love? If she could, how could anyone love her? It was the cold clouding her brain, such crazy thoughts of love—no matter, Clint would find them all. And they would each and every one pay dearly with blood and pain.

Because of her.

"I've missed you, little girl," he crooned as he revved the engine. He steered one-handed, keeping his knife hand wrapped around her body, holding her close. "We're going to have so much fun."

Now that Andre was safe, she was free to deal with Clint. The question was: how? Naked, unarmed, knife to her heart, what could she do? There was no way in hell the cops would ever catch him—despite all their planning and maneuvering and dragnetting.

This was on her and her alone. The ATV headed toward the thick forest, the cliff with its sheer drop to their right. Only one thing to do, she realized as the ground blurred beneath them.

She shoved all her might against the handlebars, barely feeling the pain as Clint's knife pierced her side. The ATV hurtled toward the cliff.

He fought her, but she bent over, focusing her weight on the controls, torquing his wrist—one of the most fragile joints in the human body. He'd taught her that.

She bit down on the exposed bit of flesh between his glove and his coat sleeve, clamping down hard until she tasted his blood.

He shrieked in fury, tried to pull his arm back, which only drove them closer to the cliff's edge. She didn't care. Her one and only thought was to hold on to the detonator. Nothing else mattered.

Clint slid his knife free from her body, not-so-warm blood slipping out behind it. He whipped the blade toward her face, but then they were flying through the air, hurtling, soaring, falling...

CHAPTER 29

As soon as Clint and Morgan sped away, Jenna abandoned her position and ran to Andre.

"Wait," Liz Harding yelled as she raced after Jenna. Their deal had been that Jenna would stay back until the cops cleared the scene.

Jenna pretended to not hear her as she sloshed through the mud and thin coat of ice. The sleet had stopped and the skies were clearing, but she didn't even notice. She skidded to a stop beside Andre, knelt in the mud, and pulled her knife to cut the duct tape that bound his wrists and ankles. "Are you okay?"

"Fine." He had his neck arched, watching past her to the action going on at the other side of the clearing. "You shouldn't be here. I don't know what the range—"

She shut him up with a kiss. "I'm damned tired of people telling me what I should and should not be doing."

The vest was nylon. She wasn't about to mess with the bomb or its ignition device, but she needed Andre out of it. She patted the back of the vest. No obvious wires.

Andre twisted around before she could slice the vest. "Jenna, don't. Let the—"

"I thought you were dead," she told him.

"We both might be if you—"

"I don't care. Can't you see that?"

Liz arrived with the bomb squad guy—one of the staties—and between them, they trundled a small containment unit, basically a cement mixer on wheels, designed to hold explosives safely.

The sound of an engine revving

screamed through the clearing. Everyone turned to look in the direction of the ATV.

"They're heading over the edge," a man's voice came through the radio. "I've lost sight of them. Repeat I've lost sight of the target."

"Anyone have eyes on Caine?" Oshiro cut in.

No one responded.

"Morgan," Andre said. "Forget Caine. Where's Morgan? Did she go over?" He started to climb to his feet, but Liz pulled him back down.

"Let us get you out of this first." She turned to the bomb tech. "Best hurry."

Jenna stood, staring in the direction the ATV had vanished, standing in front of Andre as if she could somehow magically block the signal from the dead man's switch and the bomb. *Hang in there, Morgan,* she prayed.

The tech assessed the situation and then did what Jenna was going to do anyway—he slit the vest up the back just as a loud crash boomed through the night, followed by the sound of an engine whining, then dying.

As soon as he was free, Andre stood, grabbed Jenna's hand, and they sprinted across the clearing to the cliff.

Lights from the other officers shone through the thick bramble of branches and dead trees that had been bulldozed over the edge to make room for the loggers' equipment. Ridges of granite jutted up through the dead wood, creating a nightmare of desolation.

The manhunt had now turned into a search and rescue. Officers' voices overlapped on the radio as they scrambled down and called out their findings. There was no way to climb down the steep granite cliff from the top, not without ropes and technical gear. Jenna and Andre prowled along the edge back into the trees until they found a shallow path that led down.

"I've got the ATV and Caine," a voice came over the radio. "He's KIA."

"You certain?" Oshiro asked.

"Definite. ATV crushed him. He's gone."

"The girl, find the girl," Liz ordered, her voice cracking through the night.

The path Jenna and Andre found was slick with mud and steeper than it had first appeared. As they scrambled down it, tripping over hidden tree roots and sliding in the mud, the voices on the radio kept coming.

"Wait. Shine the light—yes, pink, I see a pink coat."

"Can you reach the girl?"

Andre stopped, gripping Jenna's hand as they listened. The night felt heavy as the silence lengthened.

"She'll be all right," she told him, surprising herself by how much she wanted that to be true. "It's Morgan. She's like a cat with nine lives."

He said nothing, merely pulled her to him and hugged her hard.

"I've got her. She's—oh my God. The trees tore right through her. She's impaled on a branch."

"Is she alive?"

"She's cold, so cold. Like a block of ice. But...how the hell...she held on. Somehow the kid hung on. I have the detonator, deactivating it." His voice faded for a long moment, then returned.

"I have a pulse. It's faint, but it's there. She's alive."

CHAPTER 30

WHEN YOU FALL so fast and hard, all you can do is learn to fly.

The words kept coming, swift as swallows, elegant as eagles soaring on the wind, gentle as a breeze, harsh and hammering as a hurricane.

Morgan had no idea whose voice she heard as the black swallowed her whole. It wasn't hers. Definitely not Clint's. But it belonged to a man—or maybe men. Sometimes the words sang through her in Micah's sweet tenor, others they hummed with Nick's baritone, or guffawed and echoed in Andre's bass.

Everything she'd been told about who and what she was and who and what she could ever be had come from one man: her father. But now as she floated, blind, deaf, and dumb, her world a blank slate, she heard stories about herself, about a girl who definitely was no saint but who maybe could learn how not to be a sinner. Tales of strength and bravery. Warm wishes from people who cherished her, who had hopes and dreams for her future even when she had none of her own.

Maybe even a hint of love. Not merely the heartache of romance but also the heartsong of family.

Even Jenna's voice joined the chorus. Along with Lucy's.

Yet, still she fell. Hard and fast, hurtling through a void where time and space did not exist. Until, just as she was certain she was about to hit bottom, shatter into a million anonymous pieces, falling faster and faster and faster...and...she remembered.

She remembered. Who she was. Why she had chosen to fling herself into the void in the first place. What was waiting for her, if only she would stop falling and start flying.

So she did.

A beeping pulse as regular as the flap of a bird's wings guided her back. Someone or something was trying to tell her body when it should breathe, shoving air into her chest, but no one could tell Morgan what to do, that much she definitely remembered about herself. She coughed and sputtered and fought back, breathing when she damned well pleased, thank you very much.

She couldn't see anything. Weird, viscous jelly filled her eyes, making them sticky and blurring her vision. Her throat scratched as an invisible force yanked a tube out, and suddenly she felt free, in control—at least of her breathing. She coughed and sputtered and inhaled crisp air that blew at her and tickled her nose.

She tried to sit up, but her arms were tied down, which made her panic and flail and hit and gnash until a man's arms wrapped around her and a gentle voice whispered in her ear, "It's all right.

I'm here. It's all right. You're back. You're safe. Everyone's safe. Go to sleep now. Rest."

She wasn't sure who the voice belonged to—there were so many voices in her head, swirling like a flock of starlings—but somehow she knew he spoke the truth. She relaxed in his arms and for once in her life Morgan Ames did as she was told. She fell asleep.

In her dreams she flew, almost reaching the sun, but never so far that she couldn't make it back to earth and the people who were now her family. She was no sheep or fish or Norm...she dreamed of being a bird...but even in her restless slumber she knew the truth.

She was Morgan Ames. A girl who was sometimes a predator, sometimes a protector, but never the prey.

Morgan Ames. A girl with a bloodstained past but a blank canvas for a future.

Morgan Ames. The girl who might have given up killing for a living but who wasn't ready—not yet, at least—to give up on living.

ABOUT CJ:

New York Times and *USA Today* bestselling author of thirty-two novels, former pediatric ER doctor CJ Lyons has lived the life she writes about in her cutting edge Thrillers with Heart.

CJ has been called a "master within the genre" (Pittsburgh Magazine) and her work has been praised as "breathtakingly fast-paced" and "riveting" (Publishers Weekly) with "characters with beating hearts and three dimensions" (Newsday).

Her novels have twice won the International Thriller Writers' prestigious Thriller Award, the RT Reviewers' Choice Award, the Readers' Choice Award, the RT Seal of Excellence, and the Daphne du Maurier Award for Excellence in Mystery and Suspense.

Learn more about CJ's Thrillers with Heart at www.CJLyons.net

Made in the USA
Lexington, KY
26 September 2016